Notes, An

Notes, Anecdotes, and Billy Goats Too!

More stories for a laugh
or
to make you think

By Daniel J Lemieux

Daniel J Lemieux

Table of Contents

P. 1   **The Raft**

P. 10   **The Tank**

P. 25   **The Screams**

P. 34   **Snowbirds**

P. 46   **Snow Angels**

P. 57   **The Signs**

P. 82   **Parking Spaces**

P. 101   **What are the Odds**

P. 120   **The Moose**

P. 142   **My Train of Thought**

Notes, Anecdotes, and Billy Goats Too!

P. 158   **The Catch of the Day**

P. 172   **The Blizzard**

P. 182   **By the Seat of my Pants**

P. 190   **Before its time**

P. 201   **Just how tall was he**

P. 209   **Surprise, surprise!**

P. 218   **Trouble in the hood**

P. 228   **Eclipse**

P. 238   **The Fan**

P. 250   **The Things You Do**

Daniel J Lemieux

**This book contains three kinds of stories, fiction, exaggerated and true,
only the individuals within each story know for sure!**

Notes, Anecdotes, and Billy Goats Too!

The Raft

"Negative buoyancy occurs when an object is denser than the fluid it displaces. The object will sink because its weight is greater than the force around it."

The people you most depend on are usually the ones standing next to you. They are there when you need them, and they are there when you least expect them.

Daniel J Lemieux

Summers can be the most significant part of the year, especially when you are of school age. Some summers, you will remember forever; they make the best memories.

One such summer many years ago, my four brothers and I sat there completely drained, not from overwork but boredom. July was coming to an end, and we had already exhausted all our list of summer vacation must-dos, you know, the things we wanted most to accomplish before school started in September.

For a group ranging in ages from five to eleven, that was unheard of. We had built a fort, picked berries, and visited the Coke and Pepsi plants at

Notes, Anecdotes, and Billy Goats Too!

least a dozen times. They had tours and free samples, so we indulged so much that the guide knew us by name.

These were just a few of our plans, but now it was time for something exhilarating, time for something dangerous. The pond in the back yard was the focus of our next project. We would need to conquer the seven seas.

In a matter of hours, we had set our objectives, and we would build a raft, one that we could all sail on. Mind you, the pond back then looked to be of epic proportions. Today, not so much so.

We gathered every loose board, every log and set to work. We had nails, we had screws, and we had a rope. An old tent pole and a tarp would be our sail. All we had to do was assemble the parts.

The idea had come from having watched Huckleberry Finn's raft and Davy Crockett's keelboat on Disney or something. Everyone was going sailing, so why not us?

It took an eternity to assemble enough pieces, and then construction would begin. Back then, an eternity measured two days or less, that was if our attention span remained on the subject at hand.

Then came the sea trials; only one would take the raft out on the initial trial run. A rope tied to the raft would

Notes, Anecdotes, and Billy Goats Too!

ensure that we could drag it back to shore in the event of a disaster.

The hardest thing was always going to be who would do the initial test. Being the oldest was still a good thing; the idea was that I often got to go first. This time it was going to be different. The vote was unanimous; we would draw straws.

We realized that if one of the youngest ones chose the short straw, we would need adequate safety precautions. Once more, the launch would have to wait.

An old rusted bucket would be the bailer; why we needed a bailing bucket on a raft makes no sense now, an old innertube became the lifejacket, a whistle to signal if help

Daniel J Lemieux

was needed and a line to pull everything back. Everything was ready. It was time to go.

The moment of truth finally came; I recruited my oldest sister; she would hold the main event's straws.

"What's this for," she asked?

We were not about to tell her, Mom would have known the plan minutes later, and that would have been the end of that. So, we lied.

One of us said we were going to eat worms; we weren't sure who would go first. She laughed at us and held out the straws.

Paul drew the short straw, Conrad held out the worm bucket, and my

Notes, Anecdotes, and Billy Goats Too!

sister ran. There was no way she was watching us eat worms.

We watched to see if she was heading for Mom, but no, she headed next door to a friend's house; we were safe.

Back to the pond, we went. Chip and I held the line, while Con and Ray helped Paul put on the innertube. A hockey stick to push from shore, and off he went.

The sail was drawn and tied to the tent pole and the front corners of the raft. Slowly it drifted towards the middle of the pond. A slight breeze helped to move things along.

Now is when we usually figure out that we missed something in the design. No rudder, no way to steer. The hockey stick was too short to use as a pole the way Crockett used his on the keelboat. We had no control. The raft followed the wind and would eventually end up in the weeds.

"Quick the rope," and we all pulled at once. The raft stopped dead in its tracks, Paul was waving and whistling for us to prevent us from pulling, but of course, we didn't listen.

The rope slithered away from the raft, and we fell flat on our butts. Paul went in the other direction and then plop, he fell in the water.

At first, everyone had feared the worst, would he drown, or would he float? The innertube held, and slowly he headed for shore.

Notes, Anecdotes, and Billy Goats Too!

We were relieved, we all broke out laughing, except Paul at first, but laughter is infectious. Soon we were all in tears. This had been the funniest summer project to date. We had neglected to tie the end of the rope to the raft.

Unfortunately, the raft never returned to shore; by the next morning, it had disappeared beneath the waves. The tent pole was the only thing that we could see breaking the pond's surface.

The End

Daniel J Lemieux

The Tank

As the days went by, we would always return to the pond, the pole was still there, but we could no longer see the raft. There was more than a month before school would begin; we need another mission.

Every day we would sit on the veranda and try to dream up something bigger, better, and we would come up empty each day.

Chip had gotten hold of a comic book, Archie if memory serves me

Notes, Anecdotes, and Billy Goats Too!

right. I looked at Con, and he looked at me, and we both said, "Yes."

The others looked at us and wondered what now. By the look in our eyes, they could tell we had a plan, and one of those, oh my god, are you crazy type of a project.

The comic book's back had a model submarine that you could purchase, but it was made of cardboard and not made for the pond.

We were not about to be outdone; we needed the right material and a build location.

The plan was to begin scouring the vacant lots, the dumping spots where people threw old refrigerators and stoves. Something was bound to be of value.

One afternoon on our way back from the Coke plant, we walked by an abandoned property. We lived on the edge of town, so many such projects would often be left unfinished.

The part of town we lived in was poor, so people came and went without finishing builds or fixes. In one such place, we hit the jackpot.

Two large forty-five-gallon plastic drums were on the lot; they were going to be rain barrels. The house was partially built and had remained that way for a year.

Notes, Anecdotes, and Billy Goats Too!

Of course, we realized that rain barrels were much too small for our purpose, but they would be useful. Maybe we could connect them end to end. Time would tell.

We brought the barrels home and washed them inside and out. We removed the tops and could re-seal them in a flash.

We had a momentary lapse of reason or maybe two and decided that Niagara Falls was too far and Rideau Falls too public. There would be no going over the falls in a barrel, at least not this year.

If you strike gold, you always go back to the same mine. Off to the vacant lot, we went once more. In the back yard, they had dug a pit. In our area, a hole that size meant a septic tank.

Sitting there in the bottom was one sizeable plastic tank. It had to be seven or eight feet long, and it had two hatches. It was perfect.

The scary part would be opening the hatch. Was this a newer tank or a used one? Once more, we drew straws. Conrad drew the short one and popped the top open. It was empty and clean.

Back to the house, we went to enlist the others. We needed to carry the tank home through the backfields to avoid prying eyes.

Notes, Anecdotes, and Billy Goats Too!

We got as close to home as we could, we would need to cross the street, but it would have to wait till dark.

After supper, we headed for the yard, "Going out to play," asked Dad. "Yes," we replied. Off we went to the field. We carried the tank back to the garage and shut the door.

Dad never used the garage unless it snowed; it was our base and workshop for the rest of the year.

We popped the hatches, and in the tank, we went. It was dark, and it was hot, nothing that an extension cord, a light and a fan wouldn't fix.

We taped clocks and gauges to the walls; we had old TV parts for instrumentation panels, we even had an old telephone and a radio.

What we didn't have was a periscope. GI-Joe or some other toy company sold a collapsible periscope for a few dollars. It was time to cash in the bottles we had collected. A week later, we had the scope.

A bit of tape, a cut in one of the hatches, and it was good to go; we had a working periscope. It was time for sea trials again. Back to the pond we went. The added weight was a bit much, and we left a trail of parts along the way to the pond. We would eventually need to return for the pieces.

The tank was onshore, and this time two of us would do the initial test. I

Notes, Anecdotes, and Billy Goats Too!

was going, and so was Chip. He drew the other short straw and would be accompanying me.

Hatch open, in we went. The tank sat on the bottom. We were too heavy and in too shallow a spot for it to float. Out I went, we pushed the tank into deeper water, and it lifted like a cork. It was floating.

If you try to climb on a floating tank, it tends to want to roll away. It started to wobble one way and then another; Chip was holding on for dear life; it was like sitting in a washing machine. The tank was now too light.

Back closer to shore, up and in we went. The other three heaved and hoed, and the sub moved; if we were careful, it stayed upright. It was a balancing act.

The craft was too dangerous; it was time for a fix. We pulled back to shore, and off to the garage we went. The two rain barrels were just waiting there, almost as if they were saying, "You forgot about us."

A length of rope or two and the barrels were attached to each side of the tank. It was stable now and much easier to climb in. A bag or two of sand would also help us spread the weight around as needed.

Away we went once more. You could move around without much problem, it didn't tip, and it was bone dry. We had done it. A couple of long poles to push from shore was all that

Notes, Anecdotes, and Billy Goats Too!

we needed. Into the sub, all five of us went, a push or two, and we sailed from shore.

Every day we added things, and each day the sub sat lower in the water. It felt like a submarine. We added or removed sand to make the craft stable. Any deeper and we would submerge. Would it remain watertight if we added the extra weight?

We spent our days in the tank, coming out for meals and bed only; eventually, like all toys, it became old hat. Each time we thought about the next step, submerging. Each day we would come up with a different excuse to not try it.

Daniel J Lemieux

We needed another challenge. The pond connects to the creek and then to the river, so it stood to reason that this was our next challenge.

We cut a branch here and there, dragged the craft through shallow spots, and then the river was in sight.

The first trip would have to be a secure one; we would need to tie the tank to a tree and launch from there, a hundred feet further, it would settle in the middle of the stream held there by the current until we pulled ourselves back. Easy peasy.

We all remembered the first tiedown of the raft fiasco; this would not be a repeat performance. There were so many knots this time around that there was no way it would let go.

Notes, Anecdotes, and Billy Goats Too!

We climbed aboard, a nudge and a push, and we floated towards the middle of the river. We bobbed and swayed until the line went out. The stream held us in place. It was a success.

Getting back to shore against the current was an altogether different matter. It had taken us five or so minutes to make it out, but coming back took almost twenty. A pair of work gloves would have saved many rope burns.

The next days we came prepared; we had snow mitts, work gloves and rags, and even a few baseball mitts, no more rope burns.

Once out on the river, it started raining; at first, it was a drop or two, we shut the hatches part ways, but the air became heavy and stale. The hatch was opened once more, and then the rainwater would start seeping in. The sand in the bottom was turning to mud.

Thunder and lightning in the distance told us it was time to head back to shore. This time it took us almost forty-five minutes for the pullback to shore. We would need a better system if we were going to be out here in bad weather.

The tank was tied down, and off we went home. We knew there was an old boat crank somewhere in the garage, which might just do the trick.

It rained for two days; we were itching to get back out, but we were

Notes, Anecdotes, and Billy Goats Too!

told to stay inside each time we went to the door.

On the third morning, the sun came out, back to the river we went. The tank was gone, the rope had broken during the storm; it was nowhere.

We searched downstream for a mile or more, but to no avail. The sub was gone and probably resting at the bottom of the river.

A week went by and still nothing until Dad showed us an article in the newspaper. A homemade submarine had washed up on the shore of a small island about twenty miles downstream.

Dad had that tongue in the mustache thing going, the sign that said he was laughing without showing it.

"Whoever built this thing," he said, "Was either very smart or completely crazy."

We weren't sure if he had known it was us, and if he did, whether it was an insult or a compliment, but we giggled all the way up to bed. We knew that he knew, and that was ok with us. There would be other adventures, and they would not all end this way.

The End

Notes, Anecdotes, and Billy Goats Too!

The Screams

We have all encountered events that have profoundly marked us during our lives.

One such event happened to us thirty or so years ago. The late spring evening was a quiet one; we were next door at Dad's house sitting on the back veranda just enjoying the evening air.

Weekends at the farm was how we all referred to our parents' small house next door; it was a place of gatherings, we are nine children, and with spouses, kids, boyfriends and girlfriends, we often numbered more than thirty.

Living next door was a short walk across a small covered bridge that we had helped Dad build. The ditch was more of a runoff stream for the spring thaw than any permanent waterway.

It served as a means to cross from our property to Dad's without using the road. Drivers would often zip by at alarming speeds, and Dad or Pep, as we called him, was very protective of his grandkids; he would always make sure the kids used the bridge.

We had spent a Saturday afternoon weeding the garden. Dad did not

Notes, Anecdotes, and Billy Goats Too!

believe in a small patch. No, it was an acre or more in size, potatoes, lettuce, beans and even peanuts one year. There would be enough for all to share come fall.

There were two dozen chickens and eight piglets, and they too would be shared come winter. Dad owned twenty plus acres, most of it wooded. For those of us fortunate enough to get up at the crack of dawn, you could see the odd deer, moose, wild turkey, grouse and, of course, a skunk now and then.

There were coyotes and a wolf that would drop in during the coldest parts of winter, looking for an easy meal. The roosters would often wake us in the middle of the night. It wasn't what I would have called a silent alarm. Out we would go to chase whatever had spooked the critters.

On more than one occasion, we would be sent to the forest to round up the kids; someone had seen or heard a wolf or a wild dog. Neighbours would call each other. The party line would ring in its endless combination of short and long tones warning every household of the impending threat.

There were very few houses on our county road; you could barely see the farm a few hundred yards away. We often helped with farm chores, haying, birthing calves and in return, we would have access to the field across the road.

Notes, Anecdotes, and Billy Goats Too!

On warm sunny days, we would jump the fence with our bats, balls and gloves for a softball game; that fateful afternoon had been one such occasion.

After the game, we returned to Dad's and sat there, recounting the afternoon's exploits.

Suddenly as if an alarm had sounded, we could hear this piercing scream. Over and over, it continued.

A quick body count told us that everyone was here. Still, the screams persisted. "No, no," was what we believed we were hearing. It was shrill like the voice of a small child. Another body-count, and still, no one was missing. None of the other neighbours were close enough for us to believe that it was coming from one of their properties.

The older boys walked around the yard; it seemed like it was coming from the field where we had played ball earlier.

A small patch of trees behind the field separated the ball area from one of the farmer's fields. The noise was coming from that general direction.

The screams were horrible, almost as if a child was being tortured. We crossed the road and neared the forest; the screams were louder than ever; the younger ones told to stay home; whatever was making this noise was not for their young eyes or ears.

Notes, Anecdotes, and Billy Goats Too!

I ran home to get shotguns for my brother and me. Who or what was causing the noise would have to deal with a load of buckshot.

Every scream tore at your heartstrings; we were not ready to see what evil deeds were being inflicted on this poor child.

Half afraid to proceed, but even more to not, we entered the forest, closer and closer we crept, louder and louder was the screams.

Beyond the trees was the cornfield, taller than our group's tallest, we were going in blind. Those without firearms had axes and shovels, "stay two by two," one of us said.

Daniel J Lemieux

The corn was swaying and cracking just yards ahead of us; the screaming was unbearable.

There before us, two raccoons were in the throes of passion, noisier than a heard of screaming banshees. They turned to face us, somewhat offended by our presence. As quickly as it had started, they both disappeared through the trees to the adjoining property.

The screaming had stopped; we were relieved, happy that no one was being tortured or attacked by wild animals. We returned home, feeling oddly proud that we would have done anything to save the child in the trees, but sorry we had broken up

Notes, Anecdotes, and Billy Goats Too!

such a tender moment between consenting raccoons.

Did I say tender? Well, maybe not.

The End

Snowbirds

Back during my teenage years, I was fortunate enough to be part of a Venturers group, for those of you who are asking a what? Venturers were one step up from Scouts; the age group was fifteen to seventeen years of age.

We made life-long friends, and of course, we had a few adventures along the way. Many of our experiences were winter-related

Notes, Anecdotes, and Billy Goats Too!

ones; some still crack us up when we meet after all these years.

Here are two of our favourite stories that I would like to share, Winter Camp and Snow Angel. While others may eventually appear in these pages as well, these are my favourites.

Sometime around 1971 or 72, we suffered some of the worst winters in history, snow piled as high as the front porch's roof, one lane only on our street. These were just a few of the domino effects resulting from the extreme snowstorms we saw that year.

It was time for our annual winter camp, snow or no snow; we were headed to the great outdoors. The regional scouts association owned property up in the Gatineau Hills. This was to be our destination. Maybe we should have turned back.

Common sense should have dictated that we should have turned around and gone home on Friday night when we arrived at the last turn-off. The roads were utterly snow-covered. There were more than four feet of snow, and we still had seven miles to go.

A quick vote resulted in an eleven to zero tally; we were snowshoeing into camp. The walk would take several hours, and it was already dark. What to do?

Simple, we broke out the two small tents and set them up on top of the

Notes, Anecdotes, and Billy Goats Too!

closest snowbank. No one wanted to be in the way in case a plow miraculously appeared in the middle of the night.

The temperature was ten or more degrees below freezing, the wind was howling, and yes, we were going to sleep in tents. Within minutes the tents were up, the sleeping bags were installed, and a candle would provide all the required heat.

I must say that the night was uneventful, but the morning was here much too early. The middle of the tent had sagged at least two feet from the heat we projected. Everyone had drifted downhill, and we were one on top of the other at the base of the tent.

A quick bite to eat and off we were to camp. Three hours later, we arrived at the top of the hill overlooking the lake and lodge.

It was cold, we were hungry, but we were in high spirits, so we raced one another in snowshoes over the last mile. If you have ever walked with snowshoes, you will appreciate that running is even more challenging, especially when carrying packsacks and coolers.

More than once, we tripped over ourselves and would come up looking like polar bears or abominable snowmen. We had to dig out a few, we had to fix equipment, but we were not about to be denied

Notes, Anecdotes, and Billy Goats Too!

four feet of snow or not. We were determined to get there.

One thing to remember is that we were a bunch of crazy precocious teens. One boy had brought a bottle of rum. We each took our turn at the back of the pack to take a swig without the scoutmaster's knowledge. I shudder to think what JP would have done had he known...

We made it to camp, nonetheless. The place was small and cramped, but inside, it had a wood stove. The large cabin would be available in a day or so. Another group would be leaving later on Sunday. For now, there were eleven of us in two small rooms.

Daniel J Lemieux

Outside activities kept us busy that day; some of us carried firewood while others prepared meals, and then we would switch jobs.

The temperature dropped even lower than the previous night. We would take shifts of one hour each to maintain the stove. I would be on the two-a.m. shift.

After supper, we cleared out while the scoutmaster figured the sleeping arrangements. The three leaders would have the bedroom while the height of us shared the living area's floor.

We would be called in one by one so that the snow would not get the floors wet. This was where we would be spending the night.

Notes, Anecdotes, and Billy Goats Too!

One by one, we came in; the last two were, of course, me and another, we were senior, and we would be sleeping by the door.

I came in last; I entered; everyone looked at me as if I had three eyes. I met with the leaders in the other room. My best friend just looked at me with this odd look. Was I in trouble? Had they found out that one of the others had brought booze?

I sat on a chair and waited for the third-degree questions; all that was missing was the bright light.

"We found it," was the first thing said to me.

"Found what," I asked, knowing full well this had to do with the booze.

"Are you missing anything," another asked?

"Missing what?" I said, "I don't think so," I added.

"Go check your things," they said.

Back to the other room, I went while the others watched. I opened my sack and then looked at them and said, "Ok, give it back,"

"So, you admit that you have something missing," JP said.

"I don't think that you are funny," I said, "If you wanted bacon, you should have brought your own."

He looked at me with a puzzled look, "What do you mean, bacon," he said.

Notes, Anecdotes, and Billy Goats Too!

"You know bacon, pig parts," I answered.

"That's not what we found," said another.

"Well, that's all I am missing," I said.

"What about the magazine?" asked JP.

By now, I am getting pretty upset; what was I being accused of?

"I have no idea what you are talking about," I said.

They could see I was getting angry. Was this a prank, a joke, a test?

JP pulled out a girlie magazine and said, "This."

"You know," I said, barely able to contain myself, "That this is not mine."

"It was lying on your sleeping bag," he said.

I stood and went to the other room and looked at my sleeping bag behind the door.

"Ok," I said, "If it was in mine and you had to have laid out my sleeping bag before most of the others, right, so why did you not see it first."

They looked at each other baffled, had they neglected to follow the evidence?

"It stands to reason that you would have, would it not?" I added.

Notes, Anecdotes, and Billy Goats Too!

One of the others, my best friend, of course, owned up, "It was in my bag," he said, "And it must have rolled out as you spread them out from mine onto his," he confessed.

You always want a public apology in cases like this, but the only one that was forthcoming was from my friend. Somehow the leaders never did. On a different note, they never found the booze, some great investigators they were.

The End

Snow Angels

That same winter, our troupe needed funds; we were doing Sunday afternoon movies in the church basement, and we needed startup money.

We were renting movies and a projector, we were providing drinks and snacks at very affordable costs, but we needed the startup funds to pre-purchase some of the items.

Notes, Anecdotes, and Billy Goats Too!

The local church provided some advertisement and the hall, while we would do the rest, but how to get the all-important cash?

It's winter, and people need driveways shovelled, so off we went, five dollars here and ten there, it wasn't amounting to much, and it was backbreaking work for pennies.

One woman asked us if we did roofs; we were ready if it paid well, we had answered. She offered a hundred dollars. We now had a way of making money and lots of it.

Her roof took only thirty minutes; we had ropes; we had shovels and plenty of bodies. Two on the roof while the others took care of the accumulated snowbanks below. It was a success.

Daniel J Lemieux

The next weekend we went to Rockcliffe Park. If you know that area, it is where the Prime Minister and the Governor-General of Canada live, and it is also known locally as millionaire's row.

The word was out, and we were in business. Every Saturday, we did roofs, and on Sundays, we did movies. We had more bookings than we could do; it snowed almost every day. We would often redo the same roofs we had done weeks earlier; it just snowed that much.

The costs would go up depending on the roof size and complexity of the job. We weren't complaining.

This would be our final week; we had as much money as the troupe would

Notes, Anecdotes, and Billy Goats Too!

require for the year's activities. The big house on the street was the big tuna, the one that would pay for everything.

The people who lived on Acacia Street were well off. You could tell by the house and the three-car garage. There were more cars than parking spaces; this had to be a clue within itself.

The older gentleman was leaving as we arrived; this was a good thing because the owners would stand there on some specific jobs and tell us how to do the work. As if that wasn't enough, to please spread the snow on the lawn so they could see the street from the front door.

The lady of the house gave us the few rules and the go-ahead. The job would pay two-hundred and fifty dollars, more than double the going rate.

We set up; we had ladders against the front and back of the house; we even had access to their snowblower to spread the mass of snow that would end up in front of the garage doors.

Our troupe leader parked the owner's vehicle at the end of the driveway. She wanted to come and go as needed during the day. JP did as asked, and then we started.

Since the front yard is always the hardest because of street access, we usually did that side first. A few ropes

Notes, Anecdotes, and Billy Goats Too!

to tie the workers and shovels while those on the ground cleared the pathways as we filled them from above.

JP and I did the roof on the front of the house; they had dormers on that side, which complicated things. We had to maneuver around to prevent the lines from snagging on the dormer eaves. We always made sure that nothing would accidentally cut or catch the ropes. Large trees at the back made for secure tie-downs for our lines we were set to go.

Denis and Mike would do the backside roof as soon as we finished the front; in just over an hour, we were done, wet and tired. The other two would now set up for the back.

Up to the top, they went with ropes and shovels in hand. No one had fallen off this week, and we wanted to keep things that way. JP tied Mike's line to the only tree in the front yard while someone else tied Denis's to the back of a car in the driveway.

They began dumping the snow while we shovelled the pile at the front. The owner called JP to the door and offered to feed us; we were doing such a great job, and would that be ok. They gave us hot chocolate and cookies at other residences, so he figured sure and headed to the back to supervise the work there.

Notes, Anecdotes, and Billy Goats Too!

I had the snowblower job while three of the others were clearing the front walkway.

I went back and forth, blowing the snow to the front lawn; it reached seven or eight feet high in some places. Spring would be a mess.

As I rounded the end of the driveway, I noticed that the car's wipers were on; the owner was on her way to the store, said one of the other guys she was going to get sandwiches or something to feed us.Suddenly I could hear screaming; people were waving their arms frantically. "The car, the car," said one, "The rope, the rope," said another.

One good thing is that although it is more work, this driveway was long, like a hundred and fifty feet long. I was at the very end by the street when I looked up and saw Denis shooting up from the roof, flapping his wings like a stricken dodo bird trying to remain aloft.

The owner had not noticed the rope tied to her bumper and was leaving in a hurry; I was the only thing left between her and the open road. I waved and shouted for her to stop.She slammed on the breaks and came to a sliding stop, almost sideways while I watched Denis do his albatross impersonation only to fall from the skies into an eight-foot snowbank. Had I not been there to see the show, or had she not stopped, he would have had a three-

Notes, Anecdotes, and Billy Goats Too!

mile ride down the Springfield street hill.

It still took us almost fifteen minutes to pull him out from his head-first landing in the snow. The owner was shaken and shuddered at the idea that she could have killed him. She never resumed her drive to the store.JP escorted her back to the house while we finished up; Denis was shaken but not hurt. He spent the next half hour recounting the story from his point of view, the sudden pull upwards towards the roof's peak, and then the flight and landing.

By then, the story had become funny, and we all laughed, JP came out, and we packed up our equipment. The snowblower went back to the garage parked between the Caddy and the Bentley. JP turned and announced that that had been our last job; the previous episode had been too close for comfort. But a very profitable one.

Instead of two-hundred and fifty as promised, we were leaving with a hefty sum of five hundred dollars. The owner had felt so bad she had doubled the payout. On a lighter note, Denis only had himself to blame; the person who had tied the rope to the car was only the person who had taken flight and finished by making a snow angel, that was Denis himself.

The End

Notes, Anecdotes, and Billy Goats Too!

The Signs

As I was writing the previous story, it brought back to mind another adventure, one that some of us would just as soon want to forget.

Summer camps are very different from the winter experience. First of all, you have access to much more territory. Scout Camp is nestled between a half dozen peaks in the western edge of the Laurentians.

In the very middle is a lake, accessible by one road, which makes it a great place to let hundreds of kids loose. You watch the lake, and the way out, everything else is cut off by the hills around. It is a safe place to send your kids, and the number of activities makes it almost impossible for that nasty habit to set in boredom.

We arrived on a Friday, we would be there for two weeks> Being part of one of the older groups meant we didn't get the cabins or the better camping spots. We got the leftovers.

Our spot had barely enough space for the six tents we were setting up. The attendees were the usual ones that came for winter camp, plus those that had not, for whatever reason. Most of them were cold weather-related. They just didn't like winter.

Notes, Anecdotes, and Billy Goats Too!

The first thing on the agenda was tent assignments. The troupe leaders had the choice location while we five squad leaders each picked a tent. Once we had selected ours, we were assigned two tent mates each.

Through some magical coincidence, my group was the last one. Mike, my best friend, was away at the outhouse during the selection process. In Mike's absence, they set the groupings when suddenly he appeared out of nowhere. He was the only person left.

They rarely paired us together; it was almost a given that if I were leading squad A, he would be in C or D, never with my group. All the names had been drawn this time, and everyone had already gone with their baggage and sleeping bags.

When the powers realized this, they held a meeting; changes would need to be done to some of the teams.

"Of course," I said, "I mean, if Rob and Paul are together, that's ok, and if any of the others are, that's ok too, so why is it that," I asked.

They had no answer; the teams were fairly even, one newbie and two experienced members per group, most had two good friends, so we were no different. They finally agreed, and so the groups stayed as-is.

Many of the activities were competitive ones, canoe races,

Notes, Anecdotes, and Billy Goats Too!

obstacle courses, even a hot dog eating contest. By the end of the first week, three teams shared first place. Others still had time to make up ground during the second week.

The lake has one distinguishing feature, an island on the far side of the lake. Often it is used as a start-finish line for swimming races or canoeing. There is also has a cabin that groups can also book. Unfortunately, it too is on a first-come, first-served basis. On a few occasions, we have been fortunate enough to be the lucky group, but this time would not be one of them.

Another group of Venturers had lay claim to the island and thus had bragging rights; we competed against their groups as well our own. The grand champions would be crowned on the last full day. We still had a week to catch the points leaders.

Every so often, you try to throw the other groups off their game; we had hatched a diabolical plan. The three of us tentmates would canoe to the island in the middle of the night and make sure no one there would have a good night's sleep. There were essential points on the line the next day, and we figured they could be ours for the taking.

Quietly we slipped out of our tent. As I look back, I am sure our troupe leaders were aware we had hatched a plan. All was fair as long as no one

Notes, Anecdotes, and Billy Goats Too!

got hurt. To the canoe we went, slowly we approached the far side of the island; we had often visited the place during the previous years, so we knew the paths.

The newbie who would not be left behind was responsible for transport. He was to drop Mike and me on shore while we took care of business. Mike would swim to their dock and untie their canoes and tow them out to the other end of the island and hide them among overhanging branches away from shore.

I would act as the watch while the canoes disappeared one by one. If anyone was to come out, I would signal, and we would meet and vanish in the dark. Everything worked according to plan. I sat next to the cabin, listening. Someone was snoring while another person talked in his sleep. The others were as quiet as mice.

Almost an hour passed, and then Mike signalled, he was finished and headed to the rendezvous point. My job was to wait ten minutes and then let loose. Those ten minutes may have been the longest in my life. I couldn't stop laughing and may have chuckled loudly once or twice.

A look at my watch said that the others were ready to leave; it was my turn. I had a large branch in my hands and started scratching the wall and letting out a few growls, not loud at

Notes, Anecdotes, and Billy Goats Too!

first. I wanted one of the squeamish ones inside to sound the alarm.

I could hear voices inside, confused, half-asleep starting to ask questions, "What is that?" and "Did you hear that?" At first, the leaders said, "It's just the wind," while another said, "Be quiet and listen."

Louder and louder, I growled and pounded on the outer wall, scratching and growling.

"Bear," said one inside, "I heard it too," said another.

"Stay inside, everyone," said one of the adults.

As long as no one came out, I would milk it as long as I could. If the group didn't sleep, they would be in no shape to win the next day's final test. And so, I continued for at least a half-hour, flashlights lit up the windows, trying to see the bear.

I kicked garbage cans, and then the wind started picking up. I knew then that I had to leave; the trip back across the lake was bad enough in the dark, but waves would make things that much worse.

The trees by the cabin started swaying, and the branches continued what I had started. They were rubbing against the roof and walls, and I turned and ran.

I knew the path, and I ran like the wind and reached the meeting point. I jumped in the lake and swam the last few yards, and got in the canoe.

Notes, Anecdotes, and Billy Goats Too!

The ride back took more time than we wished, but we made it back safe and sound. Off to bed, we went.

The next morning came too quickly; our squad had slept in, we should have been up at the same time as the others. A few shouts from outside made sure we had the message; breakfast was now or never. Someone had magically given us a few extra minutes. Someone knew where we had spent the night.

The morning activities were low key, and it was almost as if they were taking it easy on us, almost too easy.

At lunchtime, we all assembled at the main camp building, the last activities would be starting shortly, and we would soon find out what would be the final trial.

Word was the group on the island had been bothered by a bear for part of the night. Making matters worse, their canoes had drifted away. Some were in the weeds while others in the brush along the edge of the island. A few of their guys had to swim out to bring the canoes back to shore.

The younger groups were assigned their tasks, obstacle course, foot races and canoe races. It was now our turn. We were brought to the edge of the lake and asked to stand in our groups.

The current overall scores were posted, and out of twenty groups, we stood in fourth place, just a few

Notes, Anecdotes, and Billy Goats Too!

behind the other three. We were within striking distance; if we finished first and the top team no higher than third, we could win this.

Now came the moment of truth. The Scout Master stood before us and pointed to the other side of the lake. At first, we thought, not swimming again, but no, he then looked higher, much higher.

"On the very top of the highest peak, there is a cross," he said as he pointed. "The object is to get to the cross, every member of your team must make it," he emphasized, "If you have an injury and cannot continue, you must bring the injured back and restart or forfeit the points," he added.

We were all shaking our heads. "This will take at least two maybe three hours barring injuries, so be careful and look out for each other," he added.

This event was going to be mass mayhem, I thought. The officials had figured this already; someone was already at the cross, we were told and would record each team's arrival times. He had the group departure times and was in contact by radio with the starters. Groups would leave three minutes apart, and spotters would watch for accidents and other issues.

We picked numbers; our team would leave seventh. We stood looking across and up; this was not going to

Notes, Anecdotes, and Billy Goats Too!

be easy. The first-place team would start in the sixth spot; at least we could keep an eye on the main competition.

The horn sounded, and group one took off a few minutes later, and two was gone, and then eventually our turn. The run around the lake to the base must be two miles through rocky terrain and brush. Team one was quickly caught by two. An ankle injury had slowed them down, but they were still trying.

"Did anyone look at what was at the base of the mountain," I asked? They both said no. I said, look for three birch trees, large ones that should be our marker to go up. Ten minutes later, we spotted the trees. We just hoped they were the right three; if not, we were toast. I looked across the lake; the last groups were getting ready to leave. It was time to make our move.

"Stop," I said, "Time to go up; if we have missed it, we won't catch the other group anyway." So up we went slowly at first. Some parts were sheer walls that you either climbed the rock face or had to go around.

Now and then, we would hear a group go by below, and we would stop and be quiet; other than the leaders, two other teams could still win this.

As soon as the groups passed, we continued. One group below had the same idea we had. We could not tell

Notes, Anecdotes, and Billy Goats Too!

which, but we were far enough ahead that we doubted they would catch us.

An hour later, we looked up; over the next ridge, you could see a pole. As we neared it, you could tell it was the cross. We hurried, our third member was lagging behind, and we waited; the whole team had to be there, and the time depended on the last member.

Five minutes later, we crossed the finish line. Other than the scorekeeper, we were alone; the other teams had not found a quicker path. Now we waited for more groups to arrive; time was still the determining factor.

Daniel J Lemieux

A few minutes passed, and another team arrived. It was the third-ranked team; they would not get enough points to stay ahead. A few more minutes and we could hear sounds from two different directions, one below and one farther along the ridge.

One team had gone further and come up by the slope while another team had followed our path. Which group would arrive first? The team coming up were fifty or so yards away while members of the first-place group were only half that distance away. They would finish ahead and win.

The scorekeeper kept watching both groups. What the leading team had

Notes, Anecdotes, and Billy Goats Too!

neglected to do was wait for their third member. He was fifty or more yards behind and would not make it before the other team's last member. Our competition finished fourth and was eventually bumped down to third place on the overall points standing.

We sat and waited for all the teams; several had turned back while only a dozen groups finished the course. Our time stood, and we won the competition. One by one, the teams headed back down. Three of our squads had made it to the summit, as had two of our scout leaders. Our other two groups were waiting at the base of the hill.

Daniel J Lemieux

As they had done for the start, the organizers did not want a mad rush back to camp, and we were asked to wait a few minutes to let the other groups clear the way.

Finally, we started down; we hadn't gone a hundred yards when we heard Rick scream; back, we went to investigate. Rick was last in line. He brought up the rear with one of the leaders; he had tripped and was in pain. Broken leg said JP, we need to get him down now.

The survival training kicks in when an emergency arises, a few branches and everyone's belts, and we had a stretcher. On it went Rick, we were ten, plus the leaders and the injured; we would need to rotate the four

Notes, Anecdotes, and Billy Goats Too!

carriers and have someone ahead to map out the best way down.

Every time I would be one of the porters, I would look at Rick and wonder what kind of face does a guy with a broken leg make? I would look at whoever was on the other side of the stretcher and sort of do a head nod for him to look at the injured. At times I would get a shrug, and other times, it was an I don't know kind of face.

We made it to the lake; the leaders had come across the lake by canoe as soon as they had heard we had finished first. The canoe was our transport back. There was only room for the stretcher and two persons, while four of us would swim alongside to ensure that the canoe did not tip. The others hurried by the path around the lake.

Rick looked way too at ease to have a broken leg; this was a scam. I was sure we were being had. The leaders must have hatched the plan. As we grew closer to shore, we could stand on the bottom; we looked at the leader and then at Rick and said, "You lied."

"It was a test," said JP, and Rick said, "It was their idea, not mine." Of course, they had picked the heaviest for their little training exercise. Those of us alongside looked at them sitting in the canoe. We dumped them in the lake and left them there.

Notes, Anecdotes, and Billy Goats Too!

They held the final presentations they gave us our medals. The other participants each offered their congratulations. Our leaders had been aware of the raid the night before; they too were hoping that one of our groups would win. They just did not expect that ours would since we'd be too tired after spending part of the night on the lake.

They all had had a good laugh with the other troupe leaders; all was fair in our little competitive world. That night we went to our tents, we were dead tired, and as soon as we sat on our sleeping bags, we realized they were full of water. We would need to find other accommodations for the night. The team we had beat out had overheard the leaders laughing. During the last campfire, they had come to our tent site and doused our sleeping bags with buckets of water.

"All was fair in our little competitive world," was all our leaders said.

Every situation became a learning experience; that was their motto. As I look back at the events, I realized that the others had overruled JP regarding the team makeup. He had concocted the broken leg scenario, and he had let slip to the other group who had raided their camp.

He had to have told them which tent was ours, especially after we had overturned the canoe he and Rick

Notes, Anecdotes, and Billy Goats Too!

were in, but in the end, we still prevailed, and it's only now I realize.

"I Should Have Read the Signs.

The End

Daniel J Lemieux

Parking Spaces

In July 1967, my father announced that he had secured for me a summer job. I was eleven and soon to be twelve. What kind of position was I offered, and who was crazy enough to hire an eleven-year-old?

Dad's family is originally from Northern Ontario, in a small place called St Charles. The village is thirty-plus miles south of Sudbury; my uncles and my older cousins were all

Notes, Anecdotes, and Billy Goats Too!

employed in one of the many mines there. Were they crazy enough to hire an eleven-year-old? Thankfully, no.

My cousin Larry was working by Inco, the copper and nickel mining company, my uncle Rodolphe would be shorthanded on the farm, and I was going up North.

I was put on the greyhound bus and shipped like a parcel. The driver asked where to, and I replied, "Hagar Ontario." He smiled and said, "no idea where that is, son, but hop on, and we'll find a drop spot for you somewhere."

The driver dropped me in North Bay, a small city on the edge of Lake Nipissing. It could have been on Mars for all I knew. I just wanted to get to Hagar. Now I know that my destination was a dozen miles from St Charles. I had visited once before, but as I said, it could have been anywhere.

The next driver for the last leg of the trip greeted me in much the same way as the previous one, except this one had heard of Hagar. I felt reassured.

The whole trip had taken almost eight hours by bus. The stopover in North Bay had added another hour of wait time. I sat in the front seat; I didn't want him to forget me, so we talked of sports much of the time.

We were both fans of the Chicago Black Hawks, and we spoke of

Notes, Anecdotes, and Billy Goats Too!

individual players like Bobby Hull and Stan Mikita and the upcoming season.

He called out the towns as we approached and dropped off the other passengers one by one. My stop was next, he said. Only a dozen miles and I would be there.

I explained I was on my way to work on my uncle's farm, and I had no idea what was awaiting me. He had laughed and said I would be fine.

The bus pulled into Roy's gas station and convenience store. I would soon find out that my uncle and my Dad's sister owned the store. They came out as soon as the bus stopped, the faces were familiar, but they were not the ones I had expected.

Daniel J Lemieux

"Rodolphe will be along in a few minutes," my aunt said; come in the store and have a pop. Not being from the area, I had no clue what pop was. I expected popcorn or something but was relieved when she handed me a Coke.

We spoke for a while, and then she nodded towards the door; my uncle had arrived. We hugged, and I told her we would probably see each other again before the summer was over.

My uncle Rodolphe is a big man, big and bald, you couldn't misplace him in a crowd if you tried. I walked to his truck, threw my stuff in the back, and hopped in the front with him. A few

Notes, Anecdotes, and Billy Goats Too!

seconds of small talk and we were off.

We passed uncle Leonard's house on the way to his place; he pointed up a side road and said that Aunt Pauline lived about six miles up that way. I was getting the grand tour.

We arrived at the farm; he stopped at the entrance and pointed to the house across the way, the one with the white barn. That's where your Dad and I and the rest of your aunts and uncles were born. It's also where we did all our pranks.

I had heard about the pranks, at least some of them, the manure pile, and the frozen cars, to name just a few. Dad had six brothers and eight sisters, fifteen kids, and I thought nine of us at home were a lot.

My aunt Jeanne was on the veranda and was waving to us; supper was ready, and could my uncle please hurry. The hired help was probably hungry from the bus ride, and that was no way to start the summer.

The first few days, he showed me the ropes, we would start haying in a day or so, and they were counting on me being on the big wagon with my cousins Joanne and Carmen. If I had any doubts about two girls helping, whatever I thought I could do, they had already done before.

We became fast friends and worked side by side in the field and the haybarn, stacking bales as high as we

Notes, Anecdotes, and Billy Goats Too!

could throw them. There was also the farm animals to care for; they owned a herd of Aberdeen Angus cows, big, black and mean.

You didn't stray too far from the fences because the bull would chase you until you either jumped the fence or climbed a tree. There were more than a few close calls that summer.

On slow days, Aunt Jeanne and the kids, me included, would drive to the back end of the property, we were going blueberry picking. We needed to go around by another county road to get there because the cows were in the pasture, as was the bull she had said.

Daniel J Lemieux

Once there, she showed us the best spots, "don't stray," she told us, "last week there was a bear, and we don't want any trouble," she explained. We each had three baskets, and we headed to the spots on the hillsides.

By lunchtime, we had filled every basket as well as our stomachs. I had never seen as many berries in one place; it was unbelievable. We would return every few days, Aunt Jeanne was making jams and jellies and pies for winter, and I could eat as much as I wanted.

My uncle informed us that we would be building an addition on the barn's rear during the next few days, "so eat because we will need all our strength," he said.

Notes, Anecdotes, and Billy Goats Too!

My birthday is on July twentieth, and she asked what I wanted; my answer was a blueberry pie. My aunt smiled and said she would make me two, both for me alone; the others would share another.

My grandmother was visiting from Ottawa. She had a gift for me, a new pair of work gloves and a hat with the Chicago emblem on it. Dinner was great, and we knew that tomorrow, the hard work would start. They weren't joking.

From morning till night, we cut trees and debarked and delimbed them. Some were squared to be used as floor beams while others would be posts.

Daniel J Lemieux

Every morning we hopped on the hay wagon to the rear of the property, and every night we returned with a load of wood. The actual construction would start in a few days.

Between the haying and the tree cutting, we did the chores that city kids rarely see, the ones that require nerves of steel and a strong stomach. A pig and a steer were tied in separate enclosures; was I bothered by the sight of blood they asked?

I knew then and there what was coming, and I replied that I was here for this part. It was farm work. We did quick business of both and returned to the other chores.

Notes, Anecdotes, and Billy Goats Too!

A few more days of construction and we finished the addition, there were still a few trees left to bring back from the back of the property, and the wagon was already there. All we needed was the tractor.

Joanne, my cousin, was outside and was sitting on the big Massey. I went over to join her for the ride. "I'm not going there; you are," she said, "I have to go to the pasture and move the cows and lock the gates," she added. I turned back to my uncle, who had a sly smile; I was baffled.

He threw me the keys to the small Ford tractor, "this is the gas lever; that's the brakes," he said.

"But there are two pedals. What is the other one for," I asked?

"No, there is a brake for each rear wheel, so press on both to stop," he said.

"But where will you be," I asked.

"I have to go to town and will meet you there," he answered.

"Don't worry, you'll be fine. Just take your time and get a feel for it. You've been there often enough; you won't get lost," he said as he jumped in the truck.

Everyone was gone; I was alone. I climbed aboard and looked at every lever and knob, and then I turned the key, a touch of gas, and it was purring. Now to go forward, there was nothing said about gears or anything. I certainly had no idea

Notes, Anecdotes, and Billy Goats Too!

about clutches and standard transmissions.

One lever on the column had the same lettering as Dad's car, P R N D S, now that made sense to me, good it's automatic. I slipped the gear into drive, and the tractor lurched forward; I was off.

The ride is a few miles, so now and then, I would speed up and then slow down, I would do turns, and I would slow down. I was getting a feel for it; this was great. If a police officer came along, would I be arrested? I wasn't old enough to drive; I had no license.

Tractors passed me and the odd car, people waved, but no one seemed to bother that a twelve-year-old was driving. Was it legal? The mailboxes along the way had names that I recognized, Robidoux, Primeau, Lemieux and more. They were Dad's cousins and other relatives; most of them were family.

Still, I drove on, feeling like a bigshot, just wait until I get back to Ottawa and tell my brothers and sisters that I drove the tractor on the road for miles all alone. I was feeling pretty good about myself.

The final turn was just ahead, slow down, stay in my lane and head for the property. What would I do if I got there before my uncle, I wondered? Was the gate open? Should I park on the road or pull in the small driveway and stop at the fence.

Notes, Anecdotes, and Billy Goats Too!

There was enough room, wasn't there between the road and fence? There ahead, I could see the wagon on the other side of the fence no more than twenty yards away.

Drop the speed and turn or no turn, I couldn't decide. Finally, I turned, stepped on the brakes, and my foot slipped between the two pedals; the gas was at the lowest setting, but each time I stepped on the pedals, my foot would slip between them.

The tractor went left, then right and left and so on. I missed the entrance and headed straight for a boulder, one half as high as the tractor. Up went the front over the boulder; still, I was pressing the brakes, and then I must have hit both.

Daniel J Lemieux

I was looking up at the sky. The tractor stalled, and I thought, this is it, I will be crushed when it flips over. I sat there for what felt like an eternity. What do I do now?

What will he say? I put the tractor in reverse and turned the key; each time I gave it gas, it would stall. I would later find out that the gas would not reach the carb in the position I was.

My uncle appeared minutes later; I was sitting on the side of the road with my head in my hands. I couldn't look at him. I had broken the tractor; it was my fault, and what would Dad say.

I could hear my uncle laughing, "that was some parking spot you found. I

Notes, Anecdotes, and Billy Goats Too!

don't think I could have done it as well as you did," he said.

He hopped on, flicked a clip that held both brake pedals together and gave a pull on the choke, turned the key and backed up off the boulder.

We opened the gate and pulled in. We loaded the wood on the thirty-foot-long wagon, and to my surprise, he threw me the keys once more and said. "The connecting clip was not set, and I'll see you back home."

He jumped in the truck, and I said, "but."

He replied that since I wasn't allowed to drive the truck and there weren't any boulders in the driveway back home, I should stop before hitting the barn.

"Oh, and turn the corners wide, there's a long load behind you this time," he said as he drove out of the yard. The brakes now worked in tandem, and all was good. The last thing I looked at before leaving was the boulder; one good thing was that it was no longer in the way.

The End

Notes, Anecdotes, and Billy Goats Too!

What are the Odds

The year I turned fourteen, many of us had decided that we were joining the Army Cadets. Every Wednesday, we would head up Montreal Road to Wallis House.

Wallis House was originally a hospital; it stood on the corners of Rideau Street and Charlotte. The 28 Service Battalion and 763 Communications Regiment and their affiliated Cadet Corps were the last units to use the building. The Cadets belonged to the Communications Group.

As I said, we met every Wednesday evening and practiced marches and drills. We took first-aid classes, and I joined the Cadet Marching Band. My instrument was the snare drum.

We participated in parades, we spent weekends at Connaught Ranges, where I first learned to shoot a rifle, but the Marching Band most interested me. Mike Asselin and Rolly Champagne made the drill marching team, and together we travelled with the group.

There were a few camp-out weekends; there were trips to winter and summer camps and band

Notes, Anecdotes, and Billy Goats Too!

rehearsals. We all looked forward to events and parades.

The summer of 1970 was the big one. I got to go to the big jamboree, two weeks at Ipperwash Army Cadet Camp on the shores of Lake Huron.

On the morning of departure, we needed to show up at Wallis House by six in the morning. The bus would leave at six o'clock sharp, no exceptions.

I awoke in a frenzy, it was five-thirty, and I had to be in full dress, uniform boots and all. I ran to Dad's room. He, too, had slept missed the alarm. Rush, rush, rush, he drove as fast as possible, but we arrived only to see the bus disappearing down Rideau Street. I had missed my ride.

Daniel J Lemieux

We pulled in behind Wallis House, and I sat in Dad's car, disappointed. I had missed a chance in a lifetime. Dad was also upset, probably more at himself than towards the bus. Two officers in full dress were coming out of the building and could see my face. If it didn't show how sad I was, nothing did.

The captain came to the car, I had met him several times during meetings and other events, and he asked why I was not on the bus.

My Dad answered that it was his fault, he had missed the alarm clock and we had just missed the bus. The officer said that the bus was full, and there would have been no room for

Notes, Anecdotes, and Billy Goats Too!

anyone else even if we had made it on time. Now I was dejected.

He looked at me and smiled, I didn't think this was a funny thing, but he said, "but you are in luck, corporal, there is a second bus leaving in ten minutes."

"Why is there another bus," we asked?

"There was no room on the first bus for the band equipment and the boxed lunches," he said, "you get to ride with the food."

The second bus came around the corner, and we loaded up, my Dad was relieved, and we were off.

Daniel J Lemieux

Ipperwash is about seven hundred kilometres from Ottawa. The ride would last more than nine hours.

As luck would have it, the five or six others on the band bus were guys I knew well; my friends had all made the first bus and would have no idea that I was coming until we arrived at Camp.

By noon, we arrived at The Trenton Air Force Base; we were to hand over meals to the guys in bus number one. There was a vacant seat on the bus if I wanted to switch but respectfully declined.

There had to be a convoy of Army buses, and we were told all of them going to Ipperwash. People were hurrying to and from buses and

Notes, Anecdotes, and Billy Goats Too!

bathrooms; it was mayhem. Which coach was which and so on?

Coincidences are odd things; you can never tell who you may come across miles from home. I sat on the bus, eager to be on our way. I didn't need the bathroom; I just wanted to get to Camp.

Now old Army buses are stuffy, and this one was no different. We opened a few windows to clear the air somewhat. Some of the guys laughed, and I think one of them was gassing up the rear of the bus.

I turned to open my window and looked at the bus next to ours. There were cadets from heaven knows where.

Daniel J Lemieux

Looking back at me was a familiar face. Charles, my cousin from Cornwall, was there trying to place the face he was looking at.

Almost simultaneously, we said each other's names. We had spent some time together a few years back at a family picnic in Cornwall. Our buses sat next to each other; both of us headed to Cadet Camp.

Had either of us been in different seats or if I had made the first bus, we might have never crossed paths.

In Ipperwash, we were twelve hundred cadets, the chances that we would have known that the other was even there were zero.

Notes, Anecdotes, and Billy Goats Too!

We spoke for a few minutes while we waited for the buses to leave on the last part of the drive, and we promised to try and catch up at Camp.

We ran into each other a few times even though we were in different barracks; we crossed paths at the beach, the parade grounds, and some meals. I think we also ran into each other at church services.

The rest of Cadet Camp was great; we learned various survival skills, map reading, orienteering, assembling and disassembling firearms, etc.

We did midnight raids on other barracks, and we got to ride in tanks and armoured personnel carriers.

Daniel J Lemieux

We practiced competitive shooting, and I had been lucky enough to win a gold medal for my group and finished in the top five cadets for the session that summer.

One day we were told to suit up, bring your outdoor gear. We are going on a hike. The equipment consisted of a change of underwear, socks and a t-shirt, a thin blanket, a hat, and a stick called the wooden gun and a poncho. Why a poncho? It was a sunny day, not a cloud for miles. I guess it was a formality.

We were dropped on a back road and given a map, a compass and a prepackaged meal that consisted of two packets of dried food, a

Notes, Anecdotes, and Billy Goats Too!

chocolate bar, two apples and two canteens of water.

We had twenty-four hours to make it to the pickup zone, unseen, and by the way, this is a competition. Good day, good night, see you tomorrow, it was noon, and we were expected by noon the next day.

Each group of six started at different intervals. We had no idea where we were and where the others were either. There were no distance markings on the map, only topography and roads. It was up to us to figure it out.

The landowners gave permission to cross private property. The only stipulations were no fires, no damages or garbage and to keep the property gates closed.

Luck would have it that another boy from Oakville and I were part of the same group. We shared a bunk in the barracks, I had the top, and he had the bottom, and now we were on the same squad.

The good thing was that we were both doing well in the orienteering and map courses. The others in the group made suggestions but were willing to follow Brad and me.

We figured the map scale from the road markings; we had twenty-five miles to go if our calculations were right. We must have marched till two in the morning before a few of the group could walk no more.

Notes, Anecdotes, and Billy Goats Too!

Someone had to have known that there would be rain that night, the ponchos, it made sense now. It started sprinkling, and it was time to stop. Where are we going to sleep? We have no tent said one.

"No need," said Brad, "take your ponchos and click the snaps from yours to your buddies," he said.

"Then use the sticks for poles," I added.

We now had tents for two. "Whoever is up first has to wake everybody. We need to be there early," one of us added.

Morning came too quickly; something funny was happening, it was still quite dark, but I could see something moving outside of the tent. Brad was looking at it too; it was still raining but more like a fine mist. Then it started; the noise was odd, not thunder, not rain or wind but mooing. Cows surrounded us, we had slept in a farmer's pasture, and the animals had come for a visit.

We were up as quickly as possible. We woke the others, changed socks. It's going to be wet, and we don't need blisters. Pack-up, it's time to go.

"It's still the middle of the night," said one of the others.

"Better go now than get stepped on by one of them," another said as he pointed to a few large ones nearby.

Notes, Anecdotes, and Billy Goats Too!

We made it first; in fact, we were there two and a half hours before the next group. We had even beat the pickup team with the trucks. Three of our guys were sleeping beside the flag that had been the destination.

"How the heck did you boys make it here that fast," one senior sergeant asked. "Did you even sleep?" he added.

"Well," answered the smallest guy in the squad, "if you had been chased by Betsy the cow for part of the way, you'd have been here early too," he said, laughing. Our team won the event, and our scores put Brad and me at the top of the class.

Some of us stayed in touch for a few years, but we grew apart like other things. To this day, I cannot remember running into any of my Ottawa friends that year at Camp. We had arrived on different buses and at different times. I was grouped in Juliette Company while they were in Echo Company.

Charles, my cousin, was in Delta if I remember well. I hadn't seen my friends for the whole time there, what were the chances of running into a cousin. I had no idea he was in cadets or that we were there at the same time? The fluke of this happening was unbelievable.

I did get to ride back to Ottawa with Mike and Rolly; we spoke of our time at Camp. They knew I had won a medal for target shooting. Their

Notes, Anecdotes, and Billy Goats Too!

Camp experience was equally fun. But neither had been lucky to medal in any event. Rolly had, he was in the grand marching band, and Mike had made the drill team. Those groups were so big that it would have been like telling an ant apart from one hundred others.

I had also medaled in map and orienteering, but I was not about to celebrate right then and there. The guys would eventually find out at the next Wednesday meeting. They were recognized for their achievements, as were all the others that had medaled or qualified for Special Team awards.

I arrived in Ottawa, and the car was waiting for us; Dad would drive all three of us since we all lived on the same street. My sister came to the door and looked at us as we exited the big station wagon. And she laughed.

What was so funny? I asked, and she pointed at my uniform pants. The bottoms were at least four inches too short. "Did you take someone else's pants," she asked?

When she stood next to me, I was now three or four inches taller than her. When I left for Camp, she had been taller; it was not so funny now. I ran into Charles a few weeks ago as we were returning from Florida. He was standing in the parking lot behind our condo, loading his car while I was unloading next to him.

Notes, Anecdotes, and Billy Goats Too!

Like Déja Vue, we sort of just smiled as if we both had remembered the last time we had been in a similar position fifty or so years ago.

We had seen each other a few times at family events between the two odd encounters, but the first and last meetings were so similar that we both laughed.

His sister Hélène lives in the townhouses next door, and he often visits as do his brothers and sisters. We are nine kids, and of course, so are they.

We have gotten reacquainted, and we speak now and then. Now honestly, what were the odds?

The End

Daniel J Lemieux

The Moose

Silly, isn't it, how things sometimes happen by accident. Several years ago, a group of us decided that we wanted to start moose hunting. We had done deer hunts and duck hunts, but moose was a whole new ballgame.

Notes, Anecdotes, and Billy Goats Too!

The location is the first and most important decision. It will dictate travel, lodging and even the minimum number of participants in the hunt itself.

I have, in other stories, spoken of my family that lives in Northern Ontario. They hunted every fall, and so we solicited their input as to location. The second hurdle is the number of hunters. Every wildlife management unit in Ontario requires a minimum number of hunters to qualify for a bull or cow tag. If for some reason, the group numbers fall short, you are put in a lottery.

We applied as a group and awaited the results of the draw. This took place months before the hunt itself.

Daniel J Lemieux

A lot of water will pass under the bridge before results are published, and tags are mailed to the successful applicants.

Family members up North were successful in their quest, and we awaited our own results. A month without a word passed, I finally called the Ministry to ascertain our fate. Everyone else had been advised but still no word.

The dreaded phone call came back with negative results. We had not individually received a tag. If only we had applied as a group, we would have been successful.

"Wait a minute," I said, but we did apply as a group. I even had a copy of the form in my hands. That year the

Notes, Anecdotes, and Billy Goats Too!

applications were sent to the nearest Conservation Office. Lucky for us, the closest was in the Larose Forest, only a few miles from my house.

I had dropped the document off myself and received a photocopy of the paper. I replied to the Conservation Officer that we had indeed participated, and we did have the required number of participants.

I returned to the Larose Forest Office and handed them a copy, which they in turn forwarded to the Ministry Office in Toronto. To make a long story short, we were awarded a Bull Tag for the zone we had applied for.

I advised the group and then the family members up North. We would be using the family hunt camp during the third and final week of the moose season.

Another group had taken our place in week two since, at the time, it appeared that we had been unsuccessful in the lottery. If we were still interested, the cabin would be vacant in the third week, we accepted.

Each member of the group confirmed their attendance; we even had an additional person join us. Being all related made things easier to plan. We had boats, we had vehicles, and now we had the cabin.

The drive up is always one of the most exciting parts of the journey. The fall colours are still something to behold. We were headed to Rush

Notes, Anecdotes, and Billy Goats Too!

Lake. We had fished here a few years earlier, so the trip into the lake was going to be an easy one. Wrong.

The logging companies were harvesting the forest in the area, and they had new roads everywhere. The old signage was gone. It was a disaster area. Miles of cut trees with a smattering of standing trees here and there, we may as well have been on the moon.

We tried this road and then that one finally met a logger, he provided directions, and we were back on track, but he warned us that beavers had dammed the road a few times and be on the lookout for washouts.

Two of us took one vehicle we were two miles from our destination, and there, lo and behold, was a newly formed pond smack dab in the middle of the trail.

We chanced a crossing, the water went up beyond the door, no time to stop here, we said. We crossed and then returned for the others. We pulled a few trees, and the water level dropped. We crossed and then headed for the lake.

We began unloading the vehicles when suddenly I had this massive cramp in my leg, I would eventually find out I had torn muscles in my calf, but that was something I would only find out weeks later. We loaded the boats and found the cabin. We patched a few holes, fixed a leaky roof and a hundred other problems,

Notes, Anecdotes, and Billy Goats Too!

but the cabin had heat, and we would be out of the rain.

We had brought two boats, so the first full day was devoted to finding hunting spots. Rush Lake is quite large, so the choices were quite numerous. My hunting companion and I settled on a small bay near the mouth of a small stream. My buddy would set up on the opposite side of a small peninsula facing away from where I would hunt.

He had the boat and me, well, I had a lawn chair. Because of my injury, I was barely able to walk more than a hundred or so yards. The chair provided me with the possibility of nestling among the tall grasses by the stream. I was dropped off and found a suitable parking spot, my chair, my moose call, packsack and rifle. I was set for the day.

There were more moose tracks within a hundred feet from my sitting spot than I had ever seen. Having lived along the Larose Forest had given me many opportunities to follow moose trails and deer trails. Here I would sit and call and watch.

I had my lunch, a bottle of water and two beers, just in case I needed to celebrate. We arrived at six in the morning, and we were prepared for the full day. By mid-afternoon, I could hear the second boat heading back to camp. The other guys were heading in.

Notes, Anecdotes, and Billy Goats Too!

I dosed on and off. Every so often, I would hear noises and would awaken with a sudden feeling of being watched. I would get up, look around, walk a hundred feet and return, just enough to wake up and then I would call and sit.

It's funny that you always worry about bears and wolves when sitting in the middle of nowhere, the hairs on the back of my neck would prop up, and I would get that eerie feeling again. I would get up, look around and sit.

On one such occasion, I stood for maybe ten minutes trying to work the cobwebs from my head when suddenly, at the other end of the bay, there was a black blotch on the beach.

I had no binoculars, just the gun sights. The blotch could be anywhere from four hundred yards to eight hundred yards, heck it could have been a mile away. I shouldered the rifle and wondered if it's that far. How high do I shoot? The previous evening one of the guys had talked ballistics. At so many yards with little or no wind, you shoot twenty-four inches higher. This was much further than what we had discussed. This was definitely a moose and a bull I was looking at.

I raised the rifle and aimed more than a body height above and took the shot. The moose was headed

Notes, Anecdotes, and Billy Goats Too!

towards my right when suddenly it turned and went left towards the forest. I emptied the clip and reloaded, and took two more shots.

I could no longer see the moose. We had debated signals if one of us was lucky enough on how we would proceed. Three of the guys were back at camp, and if they heard the gunshots, it would be an incredible piece of luck. My buddy heard the shots. He was no more than a few hundred yards away and would show up soon.

I waited and waited, but he was nowhere to be seen. Had he gone back while I had slept? Eventually, I heard the outboard coming around the point. It seems that each time I took a shot, he took cover and then would start the motor only to jump out for cover over and over, not realizing there was a fifty-foot high hill between us.

He arrived looking a bit miffed.

"What are you doing, shooting at beer cans or what?" he asked.

I kept pointing to the end of the bay, and he looked, but he couldn't see anything where I was pointing.

"Moose," I said, "I shot a moose."

"Where," he asked?

"Do you see the birch tree bent over at the end of the bay?" I asked.

Notes, Anecdotes, and Billy Goats Too!

"Yes, but you didn't try to shoot something that far. It's gotta be over five hundred yards'" he replied.

I looked at him and said, "I'm sure I hit him."

He replied, "On which shot, you must have taken at least seven or more," he said.

"Seven," I said, "One clip and two singles. The moose then disappeared from view," I said.

"He must have been bent over laughing at you," my buddy said.

"Well, let's go see," I answered.

We loaded the chair and everything else.

"Oh, by the way," I said, "I still have the two beers, so no, I didn't imagine this."

We made it to the end of the bay. He was right. It had to be over five hundred yards, but I was still determined to see.

We made it to shore, and to my surprise, there was nothing but moose tracks, hundreds if not more. I had been hoping to see a fresh set to prove my point, but they were all fresh.

"Well," my partner said, "He ain't on the beach."

"Ok," I said, "Lets both walk in the bush about fifty feet, you then turn right, and I'll turn left well walk a few

Notes, Anecdotes, and Billy Goats Too!

hundred feet and then back to shore."

There were tracks everywhere, each set fresher than the other. We did the fifty, turned away and headed in opposite directions. And then back to shore. Nothing nada. Because of my leg injury, I came back to shore somewhat later than he did. He was halfway back to the boat, and I did one of those, I don't know, kind of hunch with my shoulders.

He passed the boat and walked towards me. He was carrying a branch in one hand and his rifle in the other.

"A crutch," he said from the other end of the bay.

Suddenly he dropped the branch and pointed the gun about thirty feet from where we had walked into the bush.

"Moose, moose," he said, pointing in the trees.

"Stop fooling around," I said.

"No, seriously, he's there right there almost where we walked from the boat," he added.

"Well, shoot," I said.

"No, no, I think he's dead," he replied.

"Are you sure," I asked.

"I think so," he replied.

Notes, Anecdotes, and Billy Goats Too!

He lowered the rifle. I said, "What are you doing? Point that thing at the moose. He might just be stunned."

I arrived there, and sure enough, the moose was no more than a few dozen feet from the bent birch tree. He had fallen in a shallow hole behind tall grass, but he was there just like I had said, and he was still warm.

Panic happens fast. You don't think straight. You make stupid decisions.

"Go get the guys," I said, "I'll stay here with the moose."

"It's late afternoon, mid-October, and the sun is slowly going down," I said to my friend.

"Yes, and in an hour, it will be pitch black," he said. So off he went.

Ok, so what do I do now? Well, the moose has been down for nearly an hour and to prevent bloating, I need to bleed him, which I then began doing.

The beast had to be a thousand pounds or more. Just the head was massive. I had to flip him on his other side to finish the cut, but I had no rope, no pole, only my rifle. The next best thing is the moose's legs. So, with one front leg in one hand and one hind in the other, I started rocking him so that the momentum would eventually flip him over.

I should have let go! But no, the motion carried me over, and I went

Notes, Anecdotes, and Billy Goats Too!

with the moose. I was stuck between the legs and had got pinned in the best wrestling move I had ever seen. There I am stuck under legs, and more legs, and I can hear the boats returning. Imagine what they would have said if I was still in that position when they arrived? Lucky for me, it was pitch black.

I got out and sat on the moose, finished the cut and saw the guys rounding the bay. It was dark out, and I realized that I had left my bullets in the boat. I had been alone with a moose without any protection other than my knife and an empty rifle. I had never reloaded.

We cleaned the moose, we put him in one of the boats and brought him back to camp. It was late. It was dark, and it was cold. What to do with the moose? The solution was, leave him in the boat, anchor it in the middle of the bay and tomorrow we would deal with it.

The next day we quartered and skinned the moose, hung it in a shady place and partied the last two days. When we got up the morning after I had shot the moose, there were more fresh moose tracks fifteen feet from the cabin. No one heard him, no one saw him, but it had been here during the night.

We returned home after breaking the beaver dam once more. The ride back was done overnight, less traffic

Notes, Anecdotes, and Billy Goats Too!

and the weather was cold, better for preserving the meat.

The next day I had x-rays and an MRI on my calf. I was told I had a blood clot and a torn muscle, which they treated, and all was well. Each guy ended up with one hundred plus pounds of moose meat.

Back in the cabin the night I shot my first and only moose, we did the map math when we were at the cabin, and the guys estimated I had hit the moose at seven hundred yards. There were five bullet holes in the moose when we skinned it, one on his right side and four on the left. I had hit him with the first shot. The others were gravy.

The End

Daniel J Lemieux

My Train of Thought

I have been moose hunting on several occasions; many of these hunts have been memorable. I was even lucky enough at one time to get one. This is not that story.

A few years ago, we started a hunting club. The idea was to find a location within a day's driving distance in Northern Ontario.

Notes, Anecdotes, and Billy Goats Too!

The first year there were four of us, we had rented accommodations from an outfitter in Gardiner, a small out of the way place, twenty or so miles north of Cochrane, Ontario. Ron and his wife were running a fly-in business from the shores of Gardiner Lake.

The village had less than a dozen full-time residents but come hunting season. There would be camps along every lake, river, and bush road.

The one distinct feature was the train tracks right along the road. Every day, one or two trains would head north to Moosonee, and then they would return a day later.

You could tell it was hunting season by the number of pickup trucks strapped down on the railcars. They were heading to various outposts along the rail line.

In the eight years that I participated, we were fortunate enough to bag a moose every year but one. We were lucky enough to get two most years, and at least one year, we got three.

Perseverance always paid off. During the last years, we had grown to eight hunters. One of our group purchased an old railway office across the road. We then turned it into our hunt camp. Some of us arrived a week early, and some stayed a week later. Most years, three of us spent the full three weeks. I was retired, so I had more than enough free time.

Notes, Anecdotes, and Billy Goats Too!

This is the story of one such week when the three of us arrived early.

Every year, we purchase our licenses and apply for the moose draw. Because the group is large enough, we usually qualify for a cow tag in the zone next to the camp.

To better our chances, we always purchase two additional licenses through another outfitter, one bull and one cow tag in the zone adjoining ours.

Our system worked well, and as I have said, we have had our share of luck and a few adventures along the way. The hunt I refer to was one of our better ones; we had arrived early. There was firewood to cut and the pre-hunt cleaning of camp.

Daniel J Lemieux

Although the camp is inaccessible to mice and other animals, it does have its fair share of bugs. The cleanup of dead flies and mosquitoes would take us a full day.

There are always little fixes to do at camp, water issues to resolve, and groceries to purchase. Then the real work starts. We repair tree stands, and we build new ones.

There are usually eight of us, and often more. We follow the rules and regulations, and we are conscious of the environment.

We had planned on building a new blind down by the back of one lake where we'd had success in past years. Most of our tree stands are twenty or more feet high. We usually

Notes, Anecdotes, and Billy Goats Too!

choose spots that have an abundance of vegetation and excellent sightlines.

We had scouted the area during the previous year's hunt, cleaned a trail, and made plans. A trip to a lumber yard in town would net us the missing components, lumber, nails and rope. We were going to build the stand before the others arrived in the next four or five days.

Carrying equipment to remote locations in the bush requires the right tools. We each had an ATV, and we also had trailers and a sled. We were ready. We loaded up and drove a few miles up the logging road.

On one or two occasions, we had tried following the train tracks, but that was a recipe for disaster. The train tracks were narrow, and even if we only needed to follow it for a few hundred yards, it was a scary undertaking. Playing chicken with a locomotive will scare the bejesus out of most people. I was not immune to that fear.

We decided that there had to be a better way, we knew we couldn't use the tracks anymore, but we were allowed to cross them. The problem was that the ditches on both sides were quite deep and dangerous.

Lucky for us, the railway often leaves old rail ties here and there. We would build a ramp to cross the ditches on both sides without interfering with the rails.

Notes, Anecdotes, and Billy Goats Too!

As soon as we finished, we returned for the ATVs and trailers. Moments later, the morning train went by.

We would be safe, no rushing it, we could take our time and not worry about rail traffic. The first ATV arrived and started crossing our little ramp, a hop over the rails and then a dead stop.

The trailer hitch kept getting caught on the second rail. We got off the other ATVs and went to help.

Suddenly we could hear a train horn. It was heading our way; we couldn't see it, but there was no mistaking it, the train was coming. This situation was highly unusual, two trains within an hour.

Daniel J Lemieux

We had filled the trailer with boards of all sizes. If the train hit it, heaven knows what would happen. Would it stop in time, would it derail? We were frantic.

We started throwing the wood in the field on the other side. Still, the train horn sounded coming. Faster and faster we went when finally, the last pieces were off. We unclamped the trailer and pulled it by hand.

As soon as the ATV started moving, it fell off the ramps into the ditch. We ran and pushed it up and then ran back to our ATVs on the other side.

We hid our stuff; we didn't want problems with the railway people, and we waited. The morning's second train went by without any

Notes, Anecdotes, and Billy Goats Too!

issues. The next ATV waited a few minutes, we fixed the ramps once more, and then he started across.

Another train whistle sounded, the trains, two of them had been through there couldn't be another one, but it sure sounded like there was.

Luckily, the second ATV made it across without problems. I sat and waited while the next train would pass. It never came. After ten minutes, the other two waved to me, time to cross.

My ATV was pulling the sled; it contained the nails, the chainsaw, and the necessary tools and ladder. Just as my front wheels touched the first rail, the train whistle sounded again.

Daniel J Lemieux

We could feel the vibrations; it was coming fast. The sled's hitch pin was too long, and it hit the rail. No matter what I did, it wouldn't let me go across. I was a sitting duck on the tracks. I backed up and hit again and again, and finally, the pin bent and over the rail, I went.

Over the ramp into the field, I went at breakneck speed. I didn't stop for almost two hundred yards and finally relaxed when I was almost out of sight.

This train was a big one, a hundred cars long with four engines. It would never have been able to stop, even if it had seen us.

We eventually found out that the rail line was repairing tracks about a mile

Notes, Anecdotes, and Billy Goats Too!

up from our crossing spot, and all trains were delayed. The line was now open, the work finished, several rail trucks drove by, they ride the rails as trains do, and they carry the repair equipment, cranes, rail ties and gravel.

The whistles we kept hearing between trains were the workers flagging the trains back and forth. We did see a few more trains that day, but we were never in danger again.

We built the blind; we had our hunt, and we were lucky enough to get a bull moose from that area. On the last day of the hunt, we were bringing equipment back to camp. It was cold. There were flurries.

Daniel J Lemieux

We had to climb a hill before reaching the track crossing once more. I made the top of the hill, but the second ATV was too heavy and the hill too slick. He kept slipping back down, no matter what speed he tried.

Each of our ATVs had winches, and the big one was going to need all the power it could muster. I slid down and brought my cable down to his ATV and his winch wire back up the hill.

Tie it around the tree he had said, and he pointed to the big one nearest to me. Around went the cable, and slowly we started winching him up the hill.

Notes, Anecdotes, and Billy Goats Too!

Slowly he came up the hill when suddenly, the tree started to topple. This was a big tree. I yelled for him to jump, but the noise of the ATV and that of the winches was louder than any scream I could muster.

I looked at the tree as it was falling, and I pushed on it as it was passing by. The little bit I was able to move gave it just enough momentum for it to miss him and the ATV.

My friend looked up only to see the tree flopping just beside him. It had missed him by inches. He made it to the top, and we headed back to camp.

We had survived the multiple train crossings, but an old rotten tree had almost killed one of us. That was it. I decided then and there that I would no longer hunt on that side of the tracks. My blind was in another part of the forest, no hills, no train tracks.

It's funny what goes through your mind when you hear the rumble of the train coming, the whistle or the horn sounding as it rounds the curve just out of sight.

It is even funnier when you hear and feel the cracking of a falling tree, you have no control of the situation, and the sight becomes surreal. You try to take care of the important things at hand when emergencies arise, but that train sound really messes with your train of thought.

The End

Notes, Anecdotes, and Billy Goats Too!

The Catch of the Day

Have you ever been fishing out on the open seas, so far from shore that you might not make it back?

During the summer of 89, hmm, that almost sounds like a song's title, doesn't it? Anyway, I had been invited to Nova Scotia to do a bit of fishing.

Tom, a co-worker of mine, invited me. He's originally from Lunenburg, Nova Scotia, the home of the Bluenose II, the most famous ship replica in the Maritimes. The town is home to National Sea Products, also known as High Liner Foods.

Tom's parents still lived and owned a small tourist motel, where I was headed. I had never flown on anything before and much less been out on the ocean. These were both firsts for me, and ones I will always remember.

Every morning we would be up and off to the docks at Grey Rocks to meet our employer. Both Tom and I

Notes, Anecdotes, and Billy Goats Too!

had signed on with Normie Greek, he was a family friend, and his regular mate was off on holidays.

We were only too happy to step in, the pay, you guessed it, fish. Every day we were allowed to bring home something from the catch of the day, at least as much as the four of us could consume.

Tom's parents and the two of us had made a pact on my arrival, we would have traditional fish recipes for each meal during my stay. Breakfast, noon, and supper, it suited me as well as it did them.

Most visitors would typically forgo at least some of the meals for the more traditional breakfasts and such. I was only too happy to eat all that would be served.

Some days we brought back mackerel. Other days it was herring, hake, cod, and sole, to name a few. Tom's mother would cook twenty different fish meals during my visit, each different from the previous one.

My first days out were uneventful ones; we would leave the dock at four-thirty and head out a dozen miles or more and sometimes as much as seventeen. Some days it was foggy, some days overcast and windy, but like the meals, each different from the precedent.

Some of the days, the seas would roll. It was like riding on a camel, over one hump and then over the next.

Notes, Anecdotes, and Billy Goats Too!

We would haul in nets and pick the fish from the fishing nets like grapes on a vine. The boat, a Cape Islander, could accommodate tons of fish, and we did our best to fill its hold each day.

On the stormiest days, the boat would rise and dip broadside to the waves. We would pull in the nets, which at times appeared to come in from the sky as the boat would head up the crest of the whitecaps. Then we were pulling nets out from a wall of water that appeared as we came down the other side. It was all confusing at first, and the only time I felt seasick.

Normie would then head to the cabin and bring us each a cold beer, and things would settle down; the cure was definitely worth the effort. We would then head into the fish plant to surrender the catch.

Our boat was dwarfed by the larger ships, but everyone would drop their catches and head home.

On good days we would then head out to handline for cod. If the catch was plentiful, we would return to Normie's dock and salt down the cod for sale later.

Normie had huge barrels that he called puncheons; he could salt up to five-hundred pounds of cod in each one. They were then shipped to Halifax and Boston for sale.

Notes, Anecdotes, and Billy Goats Too!

On one such morning, we had hauled in the nets, there were thousands of fish dangling like Christmas ornaments as we lifted them to the boat. For hours we just pulled and picked.

When all the nets had been emptied, we could not believe our predicament. Normie was standing in the cabin's doorway knee-deep in fish, while Tom and I were almost buried in fish beyond our waists.

It had been so crazy that we had not had the time to look around. I was wedged in place and could only laugh. I had never seen as many fish in my whole life. Normie, our captain, had a tear in his eye, "this," he said, "has been the largest catch in my fifty-three-year career."

We had over six thousand pounds of mackerel, a thousand pounds of herring and a thousand pounds of other edible fish.

We returned to the plant, almost overloaded. We were throwing tarps over the fish to prevent them from jumping back in the water.

As we pulled in at the docks, we were greeted almost as if we were heroes. No one could believe their eyes at the sight. It took hours to empty the boat; there were fish everywhere.

We headed back out, "aren't we going home," Tom had asked?

Notes, Anecdotes, and Billy Goats Too!

"No," had said Normie, "we're going for cod if you are both up for it."

"Of course, we are," I said.

Normie explained the cycle, small fish come in, and medium fish follow, and then the bigger ones come in.

We had started the day with herring and then mackerel, and now we were after cod. There had been a few in the nets, and that was the sign our captain had been waiting for.

We threw out our hand lines, both hooks baited with fish parts and then to the bottom and start jigging. No sooner had the line hit bottom that a fish would snag the line. At times there would be fish on both hooks.

We were bringing in six fish at once between the three of us.

There were fifteen pounders and twenty pounders, there were haddocks, but most of all, it was cod.

Suddenly my line went straight to the bottom. I had a big one, foot by foot, hand over hand, I started pulling in. Bang back to the bottom, this was a fighter.

Once more, I began pulling. The others were catching left, right and centre while I struggled with my line. We had brought in a few twenty pounders, but this had to be thirty at least.

I was pooped, and we began switching between ourselves.

Notes, Anecdotes, and Billy Goats Too!

Normie would pull for a while and then Tom and then back to me. It lasted for at least twenty-five or more minutes. Finally, the line colour changed. We had a dozen feet left to bring in. Normie grabbed a gaff and readied himself, I got the fish alongside, and he hooked it.

"Watch for the second hook," he had said, "it may catch on the side of the boat." The fish was huge, "thirty-five pounds," he said. I was distracted and was watching the fish as the line moved between my fingers.

I turned to bring the line when this face appeared by the boat. A second cod was on the other hook, Normie threw me the gaff, and I hooked and dragged him in the boat. It was larger than the first cod, this one weighed-in at forty-five pounds.

We would eventually catch much more cod, but the eighty or so pounds on my line would be the heaviest that week.

We stayed out for a few more hours and returned to his dock with three thousand pounds of cod and haddock, which we cleaned and salted down. By week's end, we had filled every barrel, every puncheon that Normie owned.

Nothing was going to top this week of fishing. This would be a trip like no other. We went out one last morning, my flight back was due to leave that evening, so we helped Normie one more time.

Notes, Anecdotes, and Billy Goats Too!

"No nets today," he had said, "I have a new barrel to fill, so we go for cod again." An hour later, we were set up, and down the lines went. Up came the fish once more, Normie brought in a fifty-plus pounder, and Tom caught a flounder.

My line did the bottom trick once more, and we all looked at each other and half-smiled. I pulled, pulled, and used the capstan, a fish hauling winch, but this one was having none of it for an hour we messed with it. It would come up and then go down.

Normie gave me one of those smiles. He knew what was coming. "Is it a shark, a whale," I asked?

Daniel J Lemieux

We had seen orcas during the week. They would raid the nets every now and then. We had even pulled one up in a net until he tore a hole in it.

"No," he had said, "this won't be a whale." A dark shadow rolled and then turned white as it tried to go down again, "a halibut," he said, "and at least two hundred and fifty pounds."

The boat would angle over almost low enough to take on water. Either we would need to cut the line, or it would have to come in the boat.

He reversed the motor, and we dragged it alongside and then almost as if it had enough, in the boat it came. I had never seen a halibut in

Notes, Anecdotes, and Billy Goats Too!

my life, at least not outside of a fish market window.

Normie broke out the scotch, and we each grabbed a beer. Our last two days had been the best in our week and the best he had seen in many years.

I have photos of the cod at home and of the other catches of the day, but the halibut picture still rests in a small fishing shack in Grey Rocks, Nova Scotia, on the wall of the friendliest fisherman ever.

It seems that every catch bettered the catch of the day before.

The End

Daniel J Lemieux

The Blizzard

Many years ago, my father-in-law and I spent many a winter afternoon out on the ice, trying to catch the big one. Some outings were memorable, while others were oh-hum. Many of the oddities might be alcohol-related, not always by us, but by

Notes, Anecdotes, and Billy Goats Too!

friends or family out there over-indulging.

One such outing was on The Ottawa River. This was an all-day derby; we had a friend's ice shack, so the weather would not be a factor, at least not as long as we were inside.

Outside, things were different, below zero, with gale-force winds and blizzard conditions. If the hut had not been anchored, we would have ended up miles down-river. You could feel the shack shake. You could hear the wind whistle in the cracks in the doors and windows.

We had a kerosene stove we were set for the day. We had lunch, a few beers and maybe something a little more substantial, but we knew we would have to eventually drive home, so we didn't overdo it.

We were within one or two fish from our limit, and it was time to start thinking about packing up. Time flies when you are having a good time. One of the guys realized it was almost eight pm.

We had been out more than twelve hours, time to shut things down. I rolled in my line and packed my stuff while the others did much the same.

When I stepped outside, the wind was howling. I couldn't see the truck, and it was only a dozen feet from the shack.

A little to the left, a little to the right and then bang, I ran into the rear

Notes, Anecdotes, and Billy Goats Too!

bumper. The snowdrift had all but buried Jack's jeep. I went back in and advised the two that we would need to shovel. They laughed, so I pointed and said to them to just have a peek.

Boy, if you ever saw two guys pack up in a hurry, it was my two fishing companions. We had shovels in the shack, so John and I started clearing the snow at the back and front of the vehicle.

As soon as I would toss a shovel full, the wind would throw it back at me. This was not going to be an easy task, we thought. Jack started the truck, it barely turned over, and we had visions of sleeping there that night. Another try, and the engine sputtered and finally caught.

Daniel J Lemieux

We loaded up, and the first question that Jack asked was which way is the ramp off the ice. Everyone pointed in different directions, Great we thought, did we turn around when we arrived or were we aimed in the opposite direction from where we had come.

John, my father-in-law, said after a considerable time that yes, we had turned around to unpack near the shack. We agreed. Shore was straight ahead.

If you have seen the movies Grumpy Old Men, well, that is nothing compared to what we started to look like. When we arrived in the morning, it was a clear winter's day.

Notes, Anecdotes, and Billy Goats Too!

The shack was two hundred yards from the launch, peanuts we said.

Going back to shore was not the same thing. The lights on the truck were of no use whatsoever. There were three and four foot high drifts, go around this one, go around that one.

You now get where this is going, nowhere is where. Two hundred yards at five miles per hour should have taken no more than ten or so minutes. An hour later, we were still driving.

At times one of us would walk in front, or one would sit on the hood and just point.

Daniel J Lemieux

One side of the river is Ontario, the other side is Quebec. It's bad enough that the fishing rules and regs change halfway across. We were leery of meeting with the game wardens, but to make matters worse, the middle of the river rarely freezes completely.

Another group of friends had gone through the ice a few weeks back. They all survived the car, not so much. They were headed to the closest town for beer, case in point why we were not overindulging.

Maybe if we hadn't been so sober, we would have realized there was a problem. Every so often, you could hear the boom of the ice cracking. Even when it's three feet deep, it still

Notes, Anecdotes, and Billy Goats Too!

cracks, and the sounds will send chills up your spine.

We had no idea where we were. We couldn't see any of the other ice shacks anymore, and we couldn't see the shore. All we saw was snow and blowing snow.

If we'd had any sense, we would have gone left to find shore, but it was too late for that. Suddenly on the right, there were lights, house-lights, maybe street-lights. We stopped to investigate. If the lights were on our right, then this was the Quebec side, not Ontario. Had we crossed the river, we hadn't hit open ice. Had everything frozen over since the buddies episode of a few weeks back?

Daniel J Lemieux

I went to the closest house and asked the gentleman where we were, expecting a French answer. Britannia, he said. Now I was baffled. Britannia is on the Ontario side. We had done a complete about-face, and we were following the Ontario shore. We were three miles downriver.

The gentleman had a boat launch, which he let us use to get off the river. His last comment to us was that we would have hit the rapids and gone through the ice in another fifty yards. No one would have found us until spring. The next time we went fishing, we decided that we would leave as soon as the sun went down. If, by chance, there was a blizzard, well, we would just stay home and

Notes, Anecdotes, and Billy Goats Too!

have a few beers in the safe confines of our homes.

By the way, with all the excitement, when we got home, we all had a good laugh and promised to try again next week. Jack forgot the fish in his car, and by Monday morning, you could smell his car a block away. Maybe more like Grumpy Old Men than we thought...

The End

Daniel J Lemieux

By the seat of my pants

I'm sure he wondered what the commotion was about. They were all standing around, looking up at the tree. What were they expecting to see up there?

It had started hours earlier; we were flying kites or something like that, maybe it was the cat that had climbed the tree, whatever it was, it spelled challenge.

Dad was at work, and it had to be during the summer vacations. The

Notes, Anecdotes, and Billy Goats Too!

three of us were up to no good again. Mom would periodically check-up on us, and she would let out one of those, "I don't think so," or "Get off the roof before you fall and break your neck." If it wasn't one, it was the other.

Inevitably it would be one of the three of us getting in trouble. There was always something brewing. Whether it was uncle Rolly's camper or the garage, you would find us in, on top, or even under one of them.

By the sound of this, you would have said a bunch of terrorizing teens, but that was farthest from reality. I was eight, Conrad seven, and Paul was five, some terror right, we were misunderstood, and I'll stick with that.

Mom was getting ready for work, she did the four to midnight shift at the General Hospital, and all she was waiting for was the sitter to arrive before she would leave.

For whatever reason, I was climbing the tree. This was not some small ten or twenty-foot tree but a sixty footer. I remember crawling out on a big branch. Was I after a ball or a kite? I can't remember. There are many things from that day that I have no memory of. Fear will do that to you.

Suddenly I was hanging from the branch, swaying a dozen or more feet from the driveway, looking at the world upside down.

Notes, Anecdotes, and Billy Goats Too!

I somehow had managed to slip and fall backwards off the big branch when the back of my pants caught on the nub of a broken limb. Almost as if it had been planned, I slipped out of my pants and was dangling upside down.

The waistband had stuck to the nub, and I was dangling with only my feet still in the pants. I was secured there by the hem rolled around my ankles. My brothers were looking up at me and unable to do anything. I was at least ten feet above their heads, swaying in the wind, panicked and terrified.

One started yelling and then the other; it was bad enough to be scared out of my wits, but they were screaming like banshees.

It didn't take long for the neighbours and Mom to realize this was not the sounds coming from her sweet boys playing. Sweet right, you can go on believing that one. I had been through a few harrowing experiences earlier that summer with bees in my t-shirt and pants or the time I fell on the broken bottle and went into the house with a piece of glass sticking out of my forearm.

Mom figured, here we go again. When she made it to the veranda, all she could see was a crowd. There had to be five or six adults, most of which she had never seen before, and a half

Notes, Anecdotes, and Billy Goats Too!

dozen kids from neighbouring houses.

All of them were standing there in a circle beneath something dangling from the tree. Mom didn't need an explanation. She knew it had to be one of us. I was too high for anyone to catch me. One gentleman wanted to climb, but another said, "Don't the branch will break."

"Call the fire department," said one adult, "Get a ladder," said another. "Stop swinging," said Mom, "The branch is going to snap off." Mom missed her bus. She was standing there in her nurse's uniform; she was taking charge.

Working in a psycho ward had toughened Mom up; she was not

taking crap from anyone. Just then, Dad pulled into the driveway, everyone standing there looking up at the tree.

He wondered what was going on. The group parted, and Dad drove up and stopped right under the tree. All I remember is him looking up at me through the windshield, shaking his head, his tongue squarely on the mustache. For those who knew Dad, that was the equivalent of a full-throated laugh.

Two of the neighbours climbed on the roof car and rescued me. There I am standing with my pants down around my feet me in my tidy whities. The sitter took us into the house, and Dad drove Mom to work.

Notes, Anecdotes, and Billy Goats Too!

I wish I had been a fly on the wall because that conversation had to have been a real doozy.

That Saturday, Dad cut all the lower the tree branches. There would be no more climbing, at least not in this tree, but there were others, and we would soon be climbing them too.

I survived that episode, but the few friends that had been there teased me relentlessly about hanging there in my underwear in front of the girls next door.

The End

Daniel J Lemieux

Before its time

History, like many other things, tends to repeat itself. What was the newest trend had probably existed before in some different shape or form?

It had rained for days, and the back yard was a mess. There were so many puddles that it was beginning to look like a lake back there.

Notes, Anecdotes, and Billy Goats Too!

We had built a fort out of old doors, we had a flagpole, and we even had a flag. What we didn't have was a bridge to get from the veranda to the fort.

Every time we headed to the fort, we would have to spend our Time detouring the water holes and eventually just stepping in them. It wasn't always a problem. Sometimes a puddle needs to be jumped in, sometimes you shouldn't. That was what Mom would say if she saw us out there.

To build a bridge was out of the question; it had to be a hundred or more feet to the fort. We wouldn't be denied. If you watch enough tv or movies, there is always something that will spark your imagination.

Saturday morning, you could watch Tarzan or Bomba, the jungle boy. They had ways to get from place to place. They would swing from tree to tree and make it to wherever they were needed.

One problem we had few, if any, trees close enough to swing to and from. Believe me, we tried; a bruised forehead and rope burns were proof of some of the follies we had dreamed up. One of us swung from the veranda smack dab into the tree. And then the crying and screaming starts.

Nope, Tarzan had trees, and all we had was the veranda and the tree

Notes, Anecdotes, and Billy Goats Too!

fort. But there is always something that we had overlooked. The porch and the fort were actually connected not by land and not by sea, but by air.

The fort flagpole was Mom's clothesline post, and the veranda had the other post. I tried hanging on to the line, but it was much too hard on the fingers. I tried with gloves, and although it wasn't nearly as painful, it was a long way to the flagpole.

I tried a few times, and so did my brothers. We would never get more than a dozen feet from the veranda, and then it was a long way down to the yard. One of my brothers made it to the garbage cans and promptly fell into one.

Daniel J Lemieux

No amount of hosing down would wash the stench from his pants. How do you tell Mom that your pants are now in the garbage? I had to sneak in the house and throw a pair of pants out the window to him. It's just too bad they couldn't fit him properly. At least they were boy's pants, I said to him.

We tried holding a belt and then a rope, but it was never enough, no matter what we used. We may not be geniuses, but the next thing we tried was pure genius if I do say so myself. Once more, I snuck in the house and went to Dad and Mom's room. The top dresser drawer is where Dad kept the good stuff. He had at least four

Notes, Anecdotes, and Billy Goats Too!

pairs in there. The choice would be obvious the wide red ones.

I stuffed them in my pants and ambled on outside. If Mom saw me, she would surely have wondered what this idiot was up to, but lucky me, she was upstairs making beds. Now you are wondering what it is I snuck out with. Dad's suspenders, he wore them with everything, but the red ones were his backyard work suspenders.

This was going to be a hoot. I slung them over the bottom clothesline and clipped them to my pants, not the sanest thing I have ever done, but we were desperate. I sat on the railing and held on for dear life. A quick push from one of the others, and I was off.

I may have gone thirty feet before the clips opened up, and down I went. Partial success if only I hadn't fallen in Mom's flowers. Back to the veranda, and it was Conrad's turn. This time instead of clipping them to his pants, I tied them in a knot, and he sat on them.

A quick shove and he sailed away at breakneck speed. He managed to make it three-quarters of the way to the fort, but he became stranded there, unable to go forward or back.

We couldn't leave him there, well we could, but that wasn't cool, so I took a broom and walked to him and then proceeded to push him towards the

Notes, Anecdotes, and Billy Goats Too!

fort. If you have ever studied a clothesline's workings, you will realize that whatever is hanging on is lower than both ends.

This was starting to show some promise. The problem was the last fifteen feet. We tied a rope to his leg and pulled him the last dozen or so feet. It worked like a charm. Paul tried it, and he too made it almost to the end. This Time he had the rope, and we pulled him the last few feet.

It was my turn next. Being the oldest and heaviest was going to be a problem. Just what that would be remained to be seen. They tied the rope to my leg, and I jumped off the veranda. Being heavier had one huge plus. I was flying faster than the others had, but it also had one big problem.

By the time I made it halfway across, my feet would touch the ground. So, I ran and glided to the other end. This was great. I came back much the same way, but I believe that clotheslines stretch. When I got near the veranda, I ran right into the post.

There was blood on my face, I had split my lip and my eyebrow, I was going to need stitches. I undid the harness and ran into the house, Mom called Dad at work, and I was off to the hospital.

When we returned home, Mom was sitting on the veranda looking at the clothesline and at my accomplices. I knew I was in trouble when the first

Notes, Anecdotes, and Billy Goats Too!

thing I saw was the two of them pointing at me. I had been ratted out.

Thirty years later, we were at Dad's house next door when suddenly Eric zipped by twenty feet up in the air between the maple tree and the massive pine tree. He and the cousins had built themselves a zip line.

"Dad, look, this is the coolest," he said, "You have to try this," he added.

I looked at Conrad and Paul, who were both there visiting, and we all laughed. It took at least fifteen minutes before we were able to explain what was so funny.

I called them over and showed them the scar above my left eye and the cut on my lip that still remain, a sign that we had made this fun way before it's time. Dad then did the mustache thing. "At least, these guys didn't ruin my best suspenders doing it," he said.

The End

Notes, Anecdotes, and Billy Goats Too!

Just how tall was he

Looking back on your childhood, you can see things that may have shaped your thinking or just your general outlook on life.

My father had polio as a child; it didn't seem to me that it affected his life. It actually made him the person he would eventually become, a father to nine children and grandfather to twenty-four.

Daniel J Lemieux

Dad passed away at the age of seventy-four, much too early to ever enjoy his great-grandchildren. To date, there are about twenty- seven and still counting, and the next generation is not too far behind.

Dad had a way with kids. He had a storied childhood himself, things like blowing up the manure pile, setting the barn and cars on fire, to name just a few. There was also the other side of Dad as a child, like saving his brother from drowning when they played on the pond ice.

My grandmother once told me that polio never stopped his humour from showing itself. My grandfather once said there were too many mouths to feed on the farm. There were fifteen

Notes, Anecdotes, and Billy Goats Too!

kids in the house, so he told the kids to pick one they should get rid of.

No one said any names, so he singled out Dad. I mean, he couldn't do as much as the rest right. He only had one good leg. All the other kids stood up in front of Dad, and they all volunteered to be the one. Dad would have none of it; he was, after all, crippled and understood the numbers game.

The girls cried, and his brothers rallied and would have fought my grandfather if it came to that. Grandad said, ok if you are sure, it would mean everyone had to work just a little harder.

Grampa had heard rumblings when chores were handed out that

Norman would often not get the hard tasks. He got easy jobs because, just because, but it was never said out loud. Grampa wanted the others to realize and admit that this just wasn't the case.

The issue never came back. Dad eventually left home and moved to the city. He needed operations on his bad leg. He recalled he'd had at least twenty-two during his lifetime, and those were the ones that he could remember.

He met Mom, and that part became history. Mom asked me once if I remembered the police cars parked across the street as a child. I vaguely remembered, but it didn't raise any alarm bells.

Notes, Anecdotes, and Billy Goats Too!

Dad worked for Immigration and Manpower and had helped foil a few crises. One dealt with the Greta Munsinger affair, an East German Spy and another with another name I vaguely remembered hearing, possibly something like Ricard. He had fled Canada to Cuba during the 1960s.

The police were there to protect us since Dad had helped the RCMP trace these felons. We never knew.

But kids are cruel, we would get teased about Dad's condition, and more often than not, we would return home with bruised knuckles or split lips. We didn't win every battle, but we sure made things interesting.

Daniel J Lemieux

I remember one particular encounter. There was always the, my Dad is bigger or stronger than your Dad scenarios. One such confrontation changed much of that.

I was relentlessly teased by one acquaintance whenever he would lose at sports against us. It was his way of getting even. He once asked me if Dad could dance, and I punched him in the nose. He then asked how tall Dad was?

I replied five-eight if he stood on his right leg and five-four on his left. I'd had enough of his stupid comments and had just blurted it out. He laughed so much and said he was sorry, but if I was comfortable with his infirmity, how could he not be.

Notes, Anecdotes, and Billy Goats Too!

I once asked him how many kids in his family, and he said three. We were nine, not bad for a one-legged guy, he replied.

The End

Daniel J Lemieux

Surprise, surprise

If you have ever been, you will undoubtedly want to return. Where, well Niagara Falls, that's where.

Sue and I had our honeymoon there in seventy-five. We would return a few years later with my brother and his wife, it was summer, and we were all on vacation.

Notes, Anecdotes, and Billy Goats Too!

We stopped in Toronto, did the CN tower and a few other attractions and then it was Niagara, probably the friendliest city we have ever visited. They do tourism right in Niagara Falls. I remember our first visit, we went by Greyhound bus, we were young we didn't own a car, so on the bus, it was.

We arrived at the bus depot we called the hotel to confirm our reservation, they had nothing for us. What now? The yellow pages and the first add was the Oakes drive motel. I called, and we had a room for the week.

We would be there soon. I said we were at the bus depot, and they said we'd be there sooner than we thought. I now know why. The cab driver loaded our stuff and asked where to? When I said the Oakes, he laughed. OMG, did we pick a lemon? Were we going to the boonies, we wondered? He stopped laughing and said no worries, and pointed a block away.

OH, I now understood the sooner reference. He drove us asked if we were newlyweds, and we said yes. On the house, he said. It was a great first trip.

The second time we returned with my brother and his wife. The trip's purpose was sightseeing, so we moved around, did a bit of camping and then headed up towards Algonquin Park.

Notes, Anecdotes, and Billy Goats Too!

I was driving a seventy-six Pontiac Sunbird Coupe, not the largest vehicle for four. We had stuff everywhere, on the floors and even on the roof.

There's a police officer ahead, my brother said. We stopped, and the officer asked us to exit the car, "What's the problem officer," we asked. "Escaped convict," he said we have to check all the vehicles could we open the trunk?

I looked at the officer and said, are you serious? He was. We had ropes tying the roof rack and tent. It took almost ten minutes to undo. Have you ever seen the inside of a Sunbird's trunk? I asked the Officer, to which he replied no, not really.

Daniel J Lemieux

Inside there was one suitcase and one case of beer, needless to say, he laughed and sent us on our way. Another ten minutes of repacking and tying down, and we were gone.

If you have never been to Algonquin Park, put it on your must-do list. We set up camp, and the first night one couple cooked, the other did dishes and each day, we switched.

One evening we were on dish duty. Sue was washing. I was drying as I sat on the picnic table. Sue looked at me and said something like some people, it sounds like some old guy is making disgusting sounds in the next campsite or maybe behind our tent. My brother and his wife were sitting by the fire just having a beer when I

Notes, Anecdotes, and Billy Goats Too!

flipped on the flashlight only to see the most massive eyes looking back at me. The old guy was a big bear. Sue and I ran. The bear went for the dirty dishes.

My brother looked up and yelled, "bear." His wife sat and laughed. We were pulling her leg, she said. We weren't. She turned around, saw the bear, and in a flash, she was standing in the middle of the road. She had passed by us like the Roadrunner.

All of a sudden, all the camper's dogs started barking. The camp wardens appeared, and they chased the bear away, picked up all the garbage and left.

We returned to the campsite, and ten minutes later, the bear was back.

Daniel J Lemieux

It had been a lousy summer for bears in the area. Two boys had been mauled not far from where we were.

Our bear returned we headed for the car, the wives in back and me in the driver's seat. There was no way my brother was going around the car to get in. The bear was on that side. He dove headfirst through my window and somehow ended up sitting upright in the passenger's seat.

"Where is the bear," he asked. I looked to the right and said, "he's right beside the car look."

"No way," he said, "I'm going to freak out if I see him in the window. Lets' get out of here, he said." I wasn't about to say no.

Notes, Anecdotes, and Billy Goats Too!

So, we returned to the warden's office, and once again, they were back to chase the bear. "Don't worry, we will patrol all night," he added.

We returned once more, but there was no way we were sleeping in the tent, I said. After an hour, the wives said, see, he didn't return. Let's go to bed.

We finally agreed and headed inside the tent. I slept on one side with the axe and my brother on the other side with a machete. The brave wives slept in the middle like babies...

During the night, you could see the bear's shadow walking by the tent, the full moon casting a shadow that both my brother and I followed as he circled and eventually left.

Daniel J Lemieux

The wives just slept through it. When morning came, we had everything packed, and we were home in a few hours. There was no way we were sleeping there another night.

If you put Algonquin on the must-do list, be prepared for surprises...and bring bear spray.

The End

Notes, Anecdotes, and Billy Goats Too!

Trouble in the hood

Yes, this is another hunting story. Several years ago, a group of us were headed north on the Quebec side to chance our luck in the annual moose hunt.

We had access to a cottage along the Ottawa River. We would be hunting in the Kippawa area, just beyond the town of Temiscaming. We had brought two vehicles, one for most of the supplies and the other to use as our daily transport to and from the hunt site.

Every morning we would leave the cottage and head out to our chosen spots. The four of us would split up and spend most of the day watching trails and walking the pathways that meandered through the forest.

Much of the territory had once been pristine forest and had recently been harvested. This made for an abundance of re-growth, a virtual smorgasbord for moose. The young saplings, poplar, birch and maples attracted moose and deer. It was prime hunting territory.

Most hunters will post signs as to their whereabouts, and this place was no different. The only issue was

Notes, Anecdotes, and Billy Goats Too!

that often hunters would leave their spots at the end of their hunt and forget to remove the signage, which would confuse new hunters arriving later in the season.

One such area had been empty of hunters for quite a while, each day, we would drive by, and no vehicles would be there. There were no fresh vehicle tracks and plenty of moose and bear tracks. We finally decided that we would try our luck here. On the second day, we were having lunch when a truck came barreling down the dirt road.

Three gentlemen were in the vehicle and seemed put out by our presence there. Two of them exited the truck and started cursing and putting up such a fuss. What were we doing on their reserved spot? They asked.

We had been up and down several times without ever seeing anyone hunting and had assumed that they had gone. This was the last week of the hunt, and the place was obviously vacant.

No, they said we are here hunting. Well, the discussion went on about how much territory you could claim as your spot. They were camped miles further and declared the whole mountain as their chosen area.

In the truck, the young lad became quite upset and threatened the group with his firearm. You could see he was trying to load bullets in the chamber.

Notes, Anecdotes, and Billy Goats Too!

When the truck was approaching, I was late returning from my walk and took in the scene from the other side of our vehicle. The guys had put their rifles away while we were eating, but I was not going anywhere without my firearm like all careful hunters. I could see the young lad trying to load his gun. He was angry and agitated.

The two other gentlemen, his father and grandfather, not aware of what the lad was doing, were suddenly apprised of the situation by one of our group. Tensions were at the boiling point. No one was aware that I was standing on the other side of our vehicle with a rifle in hand. I told everyone that if the lad did not put the firearm down that, I would not hesitate to shoot if he tried anything.

The two gentlemen returned to the truck; they were both upset at the young lad's reaction. This was not how he had been taught, they both said. They removed the weapon from the lad and then explained without incident that they had been hunting there for the last two weeks and that although we could not see their vehicles at the site, they had ATVs and used back trails to access the area.

They showed us another place we could hunt, where another group had left, and things returned to normal. A few hours later, we heard a shot, one of their group had gotten

Notes, Anecdotes, and Billy Goats Too!

a moose exactly where we had been eating our lunch.

We returned day after day without much success. We packed up the trucks, ready to return home. We loaded the second vehicle, which had remained at the cottage all week.

The firearms, the ammunition, the clothing the coolers all neatly stacked. We headed out towards the highway when suddenly smoke came billowing out from under the hood. There was a fire. During the week, the wind had filled the vehicle's underside with leaves, and the heat of the engine had set them on fire. We had only gotten a few hundred yards from the cottage.

The driver popped the hood, and flames were engulfing the engine. The truck would go up in flames, the gas lines were starting to melt, we had no water, no extinguisher. We were blocking the road back to the lake.

The other truck went up the road to get water from a stream while the others emptied the van tossing everything in the bush. If the ammunition caught fire, it would be a disaster.

We returned with maybe a gallon of water. All we had was an empty windshield washer container. The others had opened a can of apple juice and doused the engine with it. The fire was out, the wiring was

Notes, Anecdotes, and Billy Goats Too!

burnt everything smelled like burnt rubber.

A jiggle on the wires here and there, and the van started up. We drove two hundred miles with the motor cover removed, and every so often, I would re-plug or jiggle the distributor wires to allow us to keep the engine running. The van made awful noises. The smell was venting directly inside the truck. It was late October, and we were driving with the windows open.

We made it to my house with the van sputtering and coughing. We smelled like a BBQ gone wrong, like roasted apples and boiled cider. Each mile, the vehicle would start acting up, and Rick still had a dozen miles before he could make it home.

I jumped in my car and would follow the van to his house. The van died three miles from home. I had a length of rope and towed him the remainder of the way.

When I think back, we could have had an incident on the mountain, only to then possibly perish with exploding ammunition and a fire that could have resulted in a faulty runaway vehicle on the road home.

Frankly, the hunt itself had been the safest part of the week.

The End

Notes, Anecdotes, and Billy Goats Too!

Eclipse

Pride is a sentiment for which there is no accurate description. It's the feeling you have inside from having accomplished something or seeing someone else achieve something that cannot, at times, be adequately explained. An eclipse is the passing of one body before another.

Daniel J Lemieux

I grew up looking at my parents, what they had accomplished during their lives and the many generations before.

Every parent wishes success upon their children. They will often forgo much to advance the chances of them attaining their chosen goals and aspirations.

My mother was the youngest girl in a family of sixteen children. She was raised on a farm in Eastern Ontario. She had younger siblings, all boys. There were twelve of them to the four girls.

She battled all her life for space and recognition and showed real determination graduating among the highest in her nursing class.

Notes, Anecdotes, and Billy Goats Too!

Among her many achievements was a perfect score in chemistry while at the University of Ottawa. I must say I wished I had done as well. Mom went on to be the head nurse in the Department of Psychiatry at the Ottawa General Hospital.

She always said that her training had paved the way for raising a family of nine of her own. A full-time job at home and one at the hospital, while many others could do neither well, was a mystery in the art of juggling that we only appreciated many years later when we had children of our own.

Dad, on the other hand, was not as academically endowed. He graduated from tenth grade and was off to work. He, too, came from a large rural family; his eight sisters and six brothers comprised a family of fifteen children nestled in a Northern Ontario farm and mining community.

Dad had caught polio at the young age of two and would require multiple surgeries throughout his life. There were no jobs around the farm that Dad would not have done and fewer still on the work stage, but medical demands needed to be followed.

On one good leg, Dad had volunteered for service in WWII and had almost succeeded. He was turned down to his great disappointment but was referred to

Notes, Anecdotes, and Billy Goats Too!

a Federal Government position by his recruiters. This was his ticket out of the farm life and into the Canadian Civil Service.

He met Mom as a boarder at my maternal grandparents' house. Both my grandparents were distant relatives, and Dad was in Ottawa for surgery and job interviews. He and Mom were destined to meet, and eventually, they were married, which is now part of history.

Both my grandmothers, Rose and Irma, often spoke of their children growing up in rural communities and how both Dad & Mom had beaten the odds that so few were able to. You could see how satisfied they both were when they spoke of all of their children's accomplishments.

As I grow older, I look at my children in much the same way as my grandparents. My daughter Miane is a case in point of overcoming and then becoming the person she is today.

Miane was a better than average student in school with lofty goals of her own. Her wish was to attend the Cordon Bleu cooking academy in Paris, which we could not satisfy as parents. Times were hard in the beginning for us, and she knew that this was an impossibility back then.

However, this did not dissuade her, and she still persisted to eventually graduate from cooking school as a

Notes, Anecdotes, and Billy Goats Too!

Pastry Chef. I can attest, as will my waistline, to her success and prowess in the culinary art. Her early exposure to bakeries had cemented her intention to pursue training, and to this day, her skills persist in the profession. Although necessity forced her to contemplate career changes, she has and still dabbles, as her family and friends will attest.

Eventually, the changes in vocation would lead her to employment in the Federal Government. Following the family tradition, you might say, is a staple in our household. Mom was a Finance Officer, Dad as a Records Manager, Grandfather in Immigration and her brother in Mail and informatics. She has ultimately outshined us all.

She now has raised her daughters to be the persons that we now see before us, and they too will one day reflect on her, as we all did on our parents. Like the choices she made, the ones they will make will bear fruit as they move ahead in life.

Miane has carried on her successes as a parent and as an employee at National Defense and now at Government Services as a Pension Specialist and at times as the Divisional Chief.

When I look back at our careers, I can only marvel at where we all were at her age and how she has eclipsed

Notes, Anecdotes, and Billy Goats Too!

both of us. There are still many stories to be written.

Her extended family now benefits from both her career choices. She still bakes and cooks up a storm and manages every task that her Management Team can throw at her.

I then turn and reflect on our grandparents and parents. I see the pride that we are all unable to explain into simple words when we look at her, as will her children when they too prepare to do the same when their turn comes.

As parents, we realized that showing our children that we approved of and encouraged them on the path they had chosen.

Daniel J Lemieux

One thing of note, Miane never really did the sports thing as a child, but the one time she did was in t-ball. That whole summer, she was the only player that never registered an out, something not even her teammate and brother could say.

The End

Notes, Anecdotes, and Billy Goats Too!

The Fan

The look in a father's eyes can often say much more than words, fathers are silent and proud, but most of all, they are your greatest fans.

Many years ago, my brothers and I played league hockey, not in a fancy arena but on outside rinks. Paul played for the Knights, and both Conrad and I played for the Bears.

Dad attended the odd game here and there. You have to remember there were no stands, no heated viewing boxes, and no benches for the fans.

Dad had only one good leg, and standing in the snow for an hour or more was something to be avoided at all costs. He did, however, attend as often as he could when the weather permitted.

If it snowed, the players would help clean the rink, we had no snowblowers, and everyone took a shovel and did their part. The kids would skate up and down in mock snowplow fashion while the parents would scoop the snow over the boards into the adjoining field or schoolyard.

The season was ending, and we were being seeded for the playoffs. The

Notes, Anecdotes, and Billy Goats Too!

Knights would face us in the first round, we would be playing my younger brother, someone would be going home disappointed.

We prevailed, Conrad scored one of our goals, and we won by a score of six to two. I played defence and rarely was involved in the scoring.

We were matched against the Aces in the semifinals. We would be facing the best goalie in the league, this guy was probably destined to play in the NHL, or so we believed. He was unbeatable.

We knew our goose was cooked. The battle raged on for three periods, we had so many chances, but Mike stopped every shot, while Marc, our goalie, was equally impressive.

Daniel J Lemieux

Marc just happened to be Mike's brother, our opponents' goalie; it ran in the family. The game went to overtime. The score was zero for both teams. The next goal would win, and the winner would head to the finals. If we were unsuccessful, it would go to a shootout, which was the worst way to lose.

During the final minutes of the overtime period, Conrad was penalized for hooking. We would be down a man for two minutes. Almost as soon as the puck was dropped, one of their better players went one on one, and I was just able to slow him down. To everyone's shock, I too, was penalized.

Notes, Anecdotes, and Billy Goats Too!

The penalty box had been snowed in, and we had to stand in the viewers' box behind our net. We were down five men to three, and they had their best players on the ice.

I felt awful; we would lose because of me, I was sure. The timekeeper let Conrad back on. He had served his two minutes; we were now five players to four, and time was running out.

The timekeeper said there was only one minute left in the game, and only thirty seconds to my penalty, we had so far held them off thanks to Marc's heroics.

I was told to get ready to jump back on, the puck was in our zone, and they were buzzing around the net as my penalty ended. Out from the box, I went. I was headed to the front of our net when the puck hit the post, and it went straight out to me.

I was not known for my skating abilities, but I went, zigging and zagging up the ice. All that was left was Mike, their goalie, and to me, it seemed that nothing else existed for a moment. He squared off and moved out to challenge.

I could barely shoot, let alone fake, so a flip to the backhand and up went the puck. This wasn't what he had expected. There was just an inch of space open above his left shoulder, the puck squeezed in, and with seconds remaining, I scored. I was

Notes, Anecdotes, and Billy Goats Too!

mobbed by my teammates; we were headed to the finals.

We eventually lost in a two-game total score final, but that semifinal game was the best. As I had walked off the ice after scoring the game-winning goal, I could see my Dad recounting to other parents every move I had made as I had gone up the ice and scored.

The fact is he had stood outside for the duration of the game. This had meant more to me than any goal that day.

That is the only goal I can remember from all the years I played, but mostly it was my father's reaction that stood etched in my mind.

Years later, I was reminiscing as I watched my son Eric who also played defence for his midget hockey team, play in a Regional tournament. Eric had won the tournament speed skating trial between games; he had posted a new speed record, and their team was headed to the finals against the boys from Arnprior.

Now our players probably averaged somewhere between five feet and six feet tall with only two of ours in the six-plus range, Eric at six-three and Patrick at six seven.

The competition was mostly all above six feet and made an imposing lineup against the smaller Casselman team. Our players were warned that these guys were big, and they were

Notes, Anecdotes, and Billy Goats Too!

mean and that they should be aware that when in the corners to be vigilant.

The game began, and the puck dropped. It was sent in our end and retrieved by Eric, who skated out with the puck. The opponents had started the game with their six most prominent players against our smaller but faster guys.

The plan was to skate faster and keep them defending as much as possible. As I said, Eric raced into the centre ice area and shot the puck to the corner of the rink and then took off like a bat out of hell.

He reached the corner just inches behind their biggest player, a lad who towered over everyone else on the ice.

A poke at the puck to get it out and then an epic collision between Eric and the giant. Down went the giant, and then Eric tossed the puck to one of our players, and he scored. Fifteen seconds in the game and we were ahead.

Everyone's jaws dropped, what had just happened. The opposing player was still on the ice and would need to be helped off. He would not return to play for a while.

Rumour from the ice was that Eric had skated by their bench and asked them who their next biggest guy was and pointing out that he was next.

Notes, Anecdotes, and Billy Goats Too!

It seems that during the pregame skate, the players from Arnprior were taking odds on who would take out the small guys from Casselman and would they have enough players to finish the game.

Casselman won the game and the tournament. Eric scored two goals from the blue line in the finals and had the hit of the game. All our players finished the game and won many of the tournament awards.

Eric had his medal from the speed skating trials, and better than that, he had in a single shift turned the odds to his team's favour. The final score, six to two in Casselman's favour. All those hours practicing while Yogi played goalie did, after all, pay off.

As Eric left the ice after the game, I could only recall the smile in my father's eyes so many years ago. I knew now how he had felt that day.

The End

Notes, Anecdotes, and Billy Goats Too!

The Things You Do

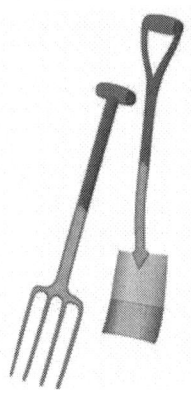

Every so often, the kids or grandkids ask you about your work, how you ended up where you did and your background. Most of them know the routine thing you did later in life, but the funny ones are the summer jobs and the first jobs you get growing up.

Someday I will not be around to tell some of these stories, so these are not your average tales but more like an overview of certain events. I just wished I had kept track of more of my own and my parent's stories and adventures

-----

I started working at the age of sixteen, I mean paid work, of course. I worked at the Notre Dame Cemetery during the summer as part of the landscaping crew.

Every morning we would tend to burial plots that required levelling, and we would fix headstones that were on uneven ground. We poured concrete, and we cut grass.

Some graves had to be dug by hand, too many large headstones would hinder the use of backhoes, so it was manual labour. There were many

Notes, Anecdotes, and Billy Goats Too!

oddities and events that stick in my mind, but none like the following story.

Jim, a friend of my family, worked with me, he mowed, and I filled holes or dug them.

One evening, we had gone to the drive-in with others to see "Children Shouldn't Play with Dead Things." Why we would see that type of film while both being employed in a Cemetery makes no sense today, it should not have made sense back then either.

Needless to say, the movie was spooky, and it had an impact on Jim. The next morning all seemed normal, I was levelling a gravesite, and he was mowing down by the water tower.

We laughed and joked about the movie when suddenly Jim's mower must have clipped one of the lawn sprinklers. He was so close to the tower that the water pressure was at its maximum. The mower started shaking, and it started going up and down, spraying water everywhere as if it was possessed.

Jim backed up, he looked terrified, and one minute later, he was running for dear life across the cemetery. He ran all the way home.

All the other guys were wondering what was wrong, I was laughing, and Jim was running. The next day, Jim didn't come to work. It took all the convincing in the world to get him to return the following week. No, the

Notes, Anecdotes, and Billy Goats Too!

mower wasn't possessed. I had to explain what had happened for him to eventually come back.

Dad worked for the Federal Government at the Department of Manpower and Immigration. A co-worker of his ran a building cleaning service.

I was hired, and two nights per week, we would be cleaning the Woolworth's and the Bank of Nova Scotia on Montreal Rd, both only blocks from my home. Eventually, we had contracts for each and every Woolworth store in Ottawa and Hull.

The best part of the job was during the summer. Two of us would clean the largest Woolworths on Rideau Street. The catch was, we worked from eleven at night until seven in the morning. We were locked in. What we most enjoyed was cleaning the kitchen. After we were done, we would cook ourselves breakfast or, the bakers who also worked nights would bring us various treats they were making for the upcoming day.

One night I was cleaning the upstairs hallways when I looked in through an open office door. The assistant manager and a female employee were engaging in acts best reserved for home. I was out of there as fast as my feet could carry me.

Every time I met the young lady during that summer, she would

Notes, Anecdotes, and Billy Goats Too!

always have an awkward smile and a red face... Funny thing though, I had never seen her face until she said sorry to me once...

At the end of the summer, I was given a bonus envelope by the manager, I had never mentioned what I had seen, and he was saying thank you in his own way.

Another summer job courtesy of another of my father's friends was as a summertime helper, I was recruited, and my jack of all trades jobs began. Some days we were doing landscaping; other days, we did odd jobs and repairs and just about every conceivable type of work that we were asked. Sam, my boss, would pick me up in his old Rambler; every day, the job would be a surprise. Today we paint, tomorrow we fix a church on Murray Street and then it was lawns on Wilbrod.

The oddest job came at the end of the summer in Manotick, a whole week at the same place near the airport. We were preparing a basement for concrete. That in itself is not the weird part. The thing was we needed to lift the oil tank off the floor and tie it to the beams above until the cement had dried.

Mr. Samson was no more than five feet tall, and that was stretching it. We had built a balancing beam much like a teeter-totter, and we needed

Notes, Anecdotes, and Billy Goats Too!

to place one end under the tank, press the other end down to lift the half-full tank.

Sam would stand on the beam; he could barely reach the ceiling. The first time he tried, his head went through the drywalled ceiling. It was much too heavy for him to hold while I would try to tie the cables. I could barely contain myself from laughing. It was cartoonish, a headless body hanging from the ceiling.

We switched places; being taller, I could press down to raise the tank high enough for him to tie it in place. I think he took his time because he had heard me chuckle. They poured the concrete that afternoon, and we returned two days later to place the tank back in its spot.

The hole was still there, and I have no idea what excuse Sam had for the owner. But one thing is certain, the scar on his head spoke volumes about what had made the hole.

I left high school in the middle of grade thirteen; I wasn't going to college or university.

I was looking for part-time work until my application to the Government was processed. So once more, I tapped into my father's acquaintances.

Zim worked for a company called Bond Brass. They made custom metal

Notes, Anecdotes, and Billy Goats Too!

parts for every type of use. They made valves for specialty uses like fire hoses and boilers, among other pieces.

The client would provide specs and a wooden model, which we would encase in a special sand mixture. We then removed the model leaving the imprint on both sides of the mould. A core piece here and there, and then we would melt the appropriate metal according to the client's wishes. Brass, copper, gold, and silver were all used daily. We then poured and let the item cool.

Once cold, we would grind, buff, package, and ship the parts. One of the more famous parts I remember working on was a bronze piece that

Daniel J Lemieux

now resides in an Ottawa museum. An outline of a man that can still be seen in a display case forty years later.

Like many other places I have worked, there was one very odd thing there. An older Polish gentleman had a unique brush that he would use to prepare the moulds he worked on. The brush was made from the locks of his dead wife's hair.

During my career, other places I have also worked for, either as full-time, part-time or on contract, include:

Taxation and Revenue Canada, Mail Room Clerk,

Canada Post, Mailman, Mail Sorter

Notes, Anecdotes, and Billy Goats Too!

Private Company, Lumberjack

Manpower Temporary Services, Jack of all Trades

Beach Foundry, Stove Assembly line

Passport Office, Records and Mail Clerk

Health Canada, Mailroom Clerk

Medical Research Council of Canada, Records Clerk

Science Council of Canada, Records Manager

Solicitor General of Canada, Chief of Records and Information Management Services

Correctional Services Canada, Chief of Information Management Services

Daniel J Lemieux

If anyone ever asks you, no, I did not work for CSIS or, as one person once said, the Canadian CIA...

The End

Notes, Anecdotes, and Billy Goats Too!

A special thanks to

my mother-in-law Muriel,

for being my most ardent reader,

and to family and friends,

you know the truth

hidden in these pages.

This publication may

not be reprinted

in part or in whole

without the author's

written consent.

DJL

Daniel J Lemieux

Books written and or Illustrated by Dan

<u>Children's Books</u>

The Seed Gatherer's Adventures

-The Pond and The Frog

-The Feather and The Hawk

-Snakes and Slides

-The Owl and The Weasel

-The Revenge of Mr. Frog

Notes, Anecdotes, and Billy Goats Too!

Adult Books

-The Seamstress

-The Keys to my Mind

-Bayou Brat

-Tuuk's Trail

-What if we had met?

-What if we had not?

-We meet again!

-With a wink and a nod

-Notes, Anecdotes, and Billy Goats

-Notes, Anecdotes, and Billy Goats Too!

Made in the USA
Columbia, SC
23 October 2023